"You clever girl," said Maggy, dropping a kiss on the little girl's straight hair. She looked at Paul.

"Isn't she beautiful, Doctor?"

"The most beautiful girl in the world." But he wasn't looking at his small patient. He bent forward, and Maggy felt his lips on hers. She stood quite still, looking at him, her cheeks very pink, but her brown eyes met his gray ones squarely.

"I don't intent to apologize, Maggy," he said, almost lazily.

Maggy forced her voice to normality. "There is no need, Doctor. I don't doubt you've kissed many a girl before me, and will kiss many more. I ken well it means nothing to you."

"Just a minute, Maggy. Are you so sure of that?"

She looked over her shoulder at him; he was standing with his hands in his pockets, looking at her with a faint mocking smile on his face.

"Aye," she said slowly, "I'm sure."

Romance readers around the world will be sad to note the passing of **Betty Neels** this past June. Her career spanned thirty years and she continued to write into her ninetieth year. To her millions of fans, Betty epitomized romance, and yet she began writing almost by accident. She had retired from nursing, but her inquiring mind still sought stimulation. Her new career was born when she heard a lady in her local library bemoaning the lack of good romance novels. Betty's first book, *Sister Peters in Amsterdam,* was published in 1969, and she eventually completed 134 books. Her novels offer a reassuring warmth that was very much part of her own personality. She was a wonderful person as well as a hugely talented writer, and she will be greatly missed. Her spirit will live on in stories still to be published.

THE BEST *of*

BETTY NEELS

A MATCH FOR SISTER MAGGY

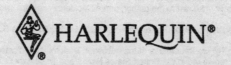

TORONTO • NEW YORK • LONDON
AMSTERDAM • PARIS • SYDNEY • HAMBURG
STOCKHOLM • ATHENS • TOKYO • MILAN • MADRID
PRAGUE • WARSAW • BUDAPEST • AUCKLAND

ISBN 0-373-51174-4

A MATCH FOR SISTER MAGGY

Copyright © 1969 by Betty Neels.

CHAPTER ONE

THE SWING DOORS were almost noiseless, but old George had been head porter at St Ethelburga's for so many years now that his ears were familiar with the faintest whisper of sound and identified it at once. He now put down his paper and peered through his cubbyhole window at the man who had just come in. A big man—a very big man; well over six and a half foot tall and broad with it; who strolled in leisurely fashion towards him. He was a handsome man too, with grey eyes, a straight nose and a wide firm mouth and dark hair, liberally sprinkled with grey. George was sure that he knew who he was; he beamed at him and said,

'Good morning, sir. Dr Van Beijen Doelsma, isn't it?' The big man, so addressed, winced slightly at the mutilation of his name by George's Cockney tongue, but smiled and nodded and said, 'Good morning,' in a pleasant voice. 'I believe I am early?'

George turned to his switchboard. 'If you'll wait a moment, sir, I'll ring Sir Charles, he told me to let him know when you arrived.'

Dr Doelsma nodded again, put vast hands into the pockets of his elegant suit, and leaned a shoulder against the wall. He appeared very relaxed—slumbrous, in fact, with eyes half closed. They flew open

5

however as his attention was caught by a figure tearing across the hospital forecourt. It was a woman, and she ran well, and he wondered why a Ward Sister in all the dignity of navy blue and white uniform needed to race around in such an unheard-of fashion. In his experience, hospital Sisters moved calmly and with a self-confident authority, designed to gain respect both from the nurses under them and the doctors they themselves worked for. The swing doors burst open with a crash, and George, waiting for his connection, looked over his shoulder, tut-tutted loudly and put his old head through his little window.

'One day you'll get caught, Sister MacFergus, running like that; you ought to know better!'

The girl came to a halt in front of the cubbyhole, and Dr Doelsma, as yet unnoticed, looked her up and down in a leisurely fashion. She was a tall young woman, well built and nicely rounded; she reminded him of the women of his own native Friesland, save for her hair, which was a bright chestnut and inclined to curl, but tidily confined in a French pleat at the back. She put up a large shapely hand and gave her starched cap an impatient tweak, and he observed that despite her haste she was not in the least breathless. She bent her noble proportions to George's level.

'Am I late? Has he come, George? Nine o'clock for a lecture! The man ought to be shot!' She had a soft voice, with a lilt of the Highlands in it. 'There's Staff Nurse off sick, and four test meals, and do send a porter over, there's someone for X-ray.' She frowned heavily above magnificent dark eyes, and her splendid bosom heaved with exasperation.

'Why are you looking at me so strangely, George? I know I'm late; I'll just have to creep in unobserved.' She paused and looked down at herself. 'Well, not unobserved, perhaps—but he'll not notice. He'll be elderly and short-sighted and fat and bald, and I'll not understand a word the poor wee man says.' She caught the faint sound wrung from Dr Doelsma's lips, and glanced over her shoulder. She smiled at him kindly and said, 'Good morning. I didn't see you. Am I keeping you waiting?' She turned back to look at George's disconcerted face and added severely, 'Don't gobble, George,' and with a starched rustle swept away round the corner of the long corridor, and out of sight.

George pushed his old-fashioned steel spectacles down his nose and peered at Dr Doelsma, and was relieved to see that the doctor was laughing softly. The sight emboldened him to say:

'Sister MacFergus was a bit worried, sir; she'd be that upset if she knew who you were—you couldn't get a nicer young lady...' He broke off as an elderly man came rather vaguely towards them. Dr Doelsma straightened and went to meet him, and the older man shook hands, smiling delightedly.

'Paul, my dear boy, I'm delighted to see you again. How is your mother?' He didn't wait for a reply, but took the younger man's arm. 'Matron's got the hall full of nurses waiting for you; shall we go before they become restless?'

The elderly doctor and his former pupil, who had carved such a brilliant career for himself, set off down one of the interminable gloomy corridors so beloved of all old hospitals. Half way down it they encountered Matron—a handsome woman with a high-bridged nose, a formidable bust, and an unshakable air of authority acquired from years of seeing that nurses did the things she wanted them to do, without being too aware of the fact. Dr Doelsma remembered her when he had been Casualty Officer at St Ethel-burga's—she didn't appear to have altered in the least. They greeted each other like old friends, and the three of them continued on their way to the lecture hall. It was familiar to them all, but even if they had been strangers to the hospital they would have found it just as easily—the subdued roar of a great many women talking could clearly be heard as they approached its doors. The sight of Matron entering, however, turned the tumult into a silence that could be felt, followed by the sound of several hundred well starched aprons crackling as their wearers rose to their feet. Matron reached the chair on the small platform and sat; the doctors followed suit, the wearers of the aprons, obedient to a nod from Matron, also sat, with a combined rustle which was deafening. The sisters were at the back of the hall; Dr Doelsma was immediately aware of the beautiful Amazon he had encountered in the entrance, sitting head and shoulders above her neighbours. Even at that distance he could see the consternation on her face—her mouth was slightly open—he wished he was near enough to see her eyes. A smile tugged at the corner of his mouth as he removed his gaze.

While Matron, followed by Sir Charles Warren, made the speeches usual to such an occasion, Dr Doelsma settled his vast bulk into his chair, and surveyed his audience. From where he was sitting most of them looked very pretty; those who were not were at least attractive, although his keen eye detected one or two really plain girls; he sighed—for the plain ones always asked questions. He had been lecturing for several years now; he knew what to expect. He supposed it was something to do with their egos. He rose to his feet, replied gracefully and briefly to the speeches and began his lecture. He was an excellent lecturer, and within a few minutes he had his audience's attention, and kept it. He made his subject, the malignant conditions of the stomach and their latest treatment, sound enthralling. He was a specialist in this field of medicine, and such was his interest and enthusiasm for his work that he had no difficulty in holding the attention of every girl there. Even the rebels, who hadn't wanted to go anyway, felt sorry for their colleagues who had been left on the wards.

Sir Charles, watching him from his side of the platform, thought what a first-rate man Paul had become. A pity he wasn't married, he mused, for he must be all of thirty-five. Too busy with his work, perhaps. It was nice for Henrietta to have such a son, though. He himself had known Paul's mother for years; his father too. Since the latter's death he had not lost contact with either of them. She would be coming over on a visit from Friesland in a few days. Behind the attentive façade of his nice elderly face, he began to make plans for her entertainment.

Matron, listening to the doctor's deep attractive voice discussing enzymes and their complex working, felt thankful that she no longer needed to know much about these new-fangled theories. In her day, a gastric ulcer was a gastric ulcer; you either recovered from it, or you died; nobody bothered with enzymes. So simple. Her massive bosom inflated on a sigh and she turned her full attention on to the nurses before her—rows of rapt attentive faces all looking at the lecturer. 'You'd think he would feel uncomfortable,' she mused, and transferred her gaze to the object of their attention, and studied him carefully. He was enough to catch the eye of any woman under eighty. He had a hawk-like distinction to crown his good looks, and as if that were not enough, his very massiveness made it impossible for him to go unnoticed. Her eyes swept the ranks of nurses before her, and she suppressed the chuckle which rose to her primly set mouth. No wonder they were all so attentive! No doubt they would all be dreaming of him tonight, and tomorrow there would be a queue of them outside her office, wanting to know if English-trained nurses were accepted in Dutch hospitals.

The applause at the end of the lecture was such that Dr Doelsma was surprised; it was, of course, more for him than for the lecture, but he was a man of little conceit, and that idea had never occurred to him. He was used to his size attracting stares, and although he had the self-confidence and assurance of a man of breeding and wealth, he was essentially modest. Now he waited patiently for the clapping to stop and then asked mildly.

'Has anyone any questions to ask?'

As he had foreseen, the plain nurses rose one by one and put their questions. They weren't particularly intelligent queries, either, but he was a kind man, and answered them in turn with a grave courtesy, leaving each of them in a rosy glow of satisfaction. He enjoyed answering the points raised by the more senior nurses and sisters; they showed a lively comprehension of his lecture and a shrewd knowledge of the subject. He had not looked at the back row since he had got to his feet; now he allowed his gaze to rest there for a moment. The Amazon of the entrance hall was in earnest conversation with her neighbour, who nodded and then got to her feet. The question she asked, 'What alternative is there to the use of vitamin B12 when both stomach and liver are diseased, making the storage of the vitamin an impossibility, and thus failing to check the anaemia?' had been well thought out. He had a shrewd suspicion as to the originator; he leaned back against the table in the middle of the platform, setting the water jug and glasses jangling, and looked over the rows of upturned pink faces, staring blandly at the big girl in the back row. Even at that distance he could see her blushing. He smiled gently and addressed himself to her.

'My answer would depend largely upon the patient. An elderly, ill patient would be best treated with palliative methods, as and when symptoms arose. But in the case of the younger person, and bearing in mind that the liver has six other functions than that of storing the anti-anaemic factor, it might be well worth attempting a liver transplant provided that the stomach condition could be controlled until such time as the resistance of the patient was sufficiently restored to warrant conservative surgery on the stomach. The hazards would be great, but in my opinion, worth while in suitable cases.' He paused, then added, 'I should like to add that this question showed a high rate of intelligence.' He didn't look at her any more after that, but after the closing speeches, followed Matron and Sir Charles out of the hall without a backward glance.

'Most successful,' breathed Matron. 'Coffee, I think, in my office.' She turned to Dr Doelsma. 'You're lunching with the consultants, I believe, but I hope I shall see you before you go.'

She led the way into her office, and they drank Nescafé, disguised in her best china. Dr Doelsma made himself very pleasant and asked a great many questions, so that after a few minutes he was able to discover that Sister MacFergus was in charge of Women's Medical. Over his second, unwanted cup, he blandly suggested that a quick tour round that particular ward would be highly interesting; there were doubtless several gastric cases there—he had remembered the four test meals. Sir Charles agreed readily enough, and politely invited Matron to accompany them. Rather to the doctors' surprise, she accepted with alacrity, and at once swept them out and away and up a series of staircases which eventually brought them on to the landing outside Women's Medical.

Their arrival was seen only by a small junior nurse, who looked at them in patent horror and scuttled, head down, to a door marked 'Sister's Office', where she knocked and entered. Dr Doelsma's lips twitched, but he avoided Sir Charles' amused look, and remarked politely upon the tasteful display of flowers on the window ledge. He turned from their contemplation in time to see Sister MacFergus emerge from her office. She looked cool and dignified, concealing the faint unease she was feeling. She addressed herself politely to Matron, and waited to hear what was wanted of her. She had smiled warmly at Sir Charles, who smiled back, but she carefully avoided the visiting doctor's eye.

'Sister MacFergus, this is Dr Doelsma. You were, of course, at his lecture. He would like to go round your ward—you have several gastrics. I believe?'

Sister MacFergus offered a hand, wordlessly, and raised her brown eyes to his grey ones in an unsmiling face, acknowledging his greeting with an inclination of her head. Of the fact that her heart was beating a tumultuous tattoo as his hand engulfed hers, she gave no sign. She turned to Matron.

'The ward's a wee bit untidy, Matron. Staff Nurse Williams is off sick with a raging toothache, the puir lass.'

'Oh, I forgot that, Sister. Perhaps it would be as well if we postponed our visit.' Matron glanced at Dr

Doelsma, who flicked an infinitesimal speck off a beautifully tailored sleeve, remarking,

'Yes, of course—I must apologise for taking you unawares, Sister. I don't wish to add to your difficulties; doubtless you have more than you can cope with already.'

Sister MacFergus fancied that she detected derision in his voice. This had the immediate effect of causing her to say in a level voice,

'Thank you, sir, but I believe we will manage very well.' She turned her head and raised her voice slightly and called to the same little nurse whom they had first seen, and who now came trotting out of the office, listened to low-voiced instructions, cast her Ward Sister a look of devotion and made off.

They all heard the whispered warning, 'Don't run, Nurse!' But Sister MacFergus, aware of the strong views authority held regarding running nurses, caught Matron's eye and said before that lady could speak,

'Yon's a guid wee lass, and willing, Matron.' She stepped back so that Matron and Sir Charles could precede her through the door into the ward. There was a brief glimpse of bedpans being whisked into the sluice at the far end, and a nurse was coming at a brisk pace down the ward towards them. She bobbed her head at Matron and Sir Charles, and made eyes at Dr Doelsma before asking, 'Yes, Sister?' in a breathless whisper.

Sister MacFergus spoke unhurriedly. 'All the gastric X-rays, Nurse, and the notes, and make sure the patients are ready for examination. There's no time to get Mrs Burt ready, but you should have time to see to the others—be as quiet as you can.' She gave a smiling nod, and the nurse, with another look at Dr Doelsma, slipped away, leaving him standing with Sister MacFergus in the doorway.

'Allow me to compliment you on your ward, Sister; I see that you are indeed able to cope with any situation.' He paused, and when she looked at him, went on in a silky voice. 'Even the unexpected visit of a fat, elderly balding and near-sighted Dutchman.'

He smiled at her charmingly, and murmured. 'After you, Sister,' and she walked ahead of him into the ward, brown eyes flashing, head very high, and cheeks scarlet.

The round went smoothly. Dr Doelsma found himself with Matron, and when he at length contrived to get near the other two, it was to observe that they seemed on friendly terms—indeed. Sir Charles was calling Sister MacFergus Maggy without any objection on her part. With a little ingenuity, the doctor contrived to change places with Sir Charles, and conversed pleasantly enough between the beds.

'That was a very good question you put at the end of my lecture, Sister.'

Maggy MacFergus was taken completely off her guard. 'Thank you, Doctor. I have a patient with that very condition which you mentioned—Mrs Salt.' She stopped and looked at him enquiringly. 'Who told you it was my question?'

'No one. I have good eyesight, and I happened to be looking at the back row.'

They had reached Mrs Salt's bed; an old lady with black boot-button eyes and ill-fitting dentures. She had been in hospital for a long time and was regarded by the entire staff as a kind of ward mascot, whose elderly tantrums were to be cheerfully endured. She greeted Matron and Sir Charles in a piping voice and wasted no more time on them. Instead, she turned her gaze on Sister MacFergus.

'Ullo, dearie. Now that's what I like to see—a well-matched pair. And about time too; a nice girl like you going begging, Sister.'

Sister MacFergus, with great strength of mind, ignored this awful remark, merely saying in a repressive voice,

'Dr Doelsma would like to ask you a few questions. Mrs Salt.'

Mrs Salt turned her naughty old face up to his.

'And I'll answer 'em. Haven't seen such a 'andsome face for years. Just the right size for Sister too.' She grinned, well pleased with herself, and Dr Doelsma chuckled and sat down on the side of her bed and took one of her old hands in his; it felt quite weightless.

'I see that you are a great one for a joke, Mrs Salt.'

'I like a good larf—How come you speak English like us?' she queried.

'I went to school,' he answered gravely. 'And now, Mrs Salt, oblige me by putting out your tongue.'

She complied promptly, and answered his questions cheerfully enough, and when he had finished he

got up, shook hands, and hoped that he would see her
again the next time he came.

'Yer'd better 'urry up, then, Doctor. I'll be ninety
in October.' She clutched his hand. 'And I bet it
won't be me yer'll come to see.' She nodded and
winked and jerked her thumb in the direction of Sister
MacFergus, who, beyond going rather pink, and
breathing loudly, ignored her. Mrs Salt looked disappointed at this poor response to her sally, and said
resignedly,

'Now I suppose you're going to talk to old sour-
face.' She jerked her head at the next bed, where a
dark-haired woman with sallow skin and a sullen expression lay watching them. But Matron, who had
looked at her watch, decreed otherwise. If the doctors
were to go to their luncheon as arranged, they should
leave the ward at once.

They all walked to the door, where farewells, gracious on Matron's part, friendly on Sir Charles' and
casual on the part of Dr Doelsma, were said, and the
visitors began their descent of the stairs. On the first
half-landing, however, Dr Doelsma stopped, and said
thoughtfully,

'I remember now, there was something I wished to
say to Sister—it quite slipped my mind on the ward.
You will forgive me if I go back? I won't be above
a minute or two.'

He went upstairs again, three steps at a time, to
find the landing empty and Sister's door shut. He
knocked without hesitation, and went in. Sister
MacFergus was standing by her desk, doing nothing.

The nurse who had eyed him in the ward was rattling cups and saucers on a tray. They both looked up, astonished, as he went in. The astonishment on Sister MacFergus's face, however, quickly turned to a heavy frown which she made no attempt to hide. The doctor, it seemed, was impervious to cross looks, for he merely held the door open, remarking,

'Perhaps Nurse could leave us for a moment? A small matter, purely between ourselves, Sister.'

The nurse smiled at him, and then looked at Sister MacFergus, who gave a brief nod of assent. As the girl slipped away through the door, she flashed beautiful green eyes at the doctor, and was rewarded by an appreciative stare as he shut the door behind her, and leaned against it with his hands in his pockets. Maggy MacFergus stood where she was, looking at him, her brows still drawn together in a thick line.

'What do you want?' she asked at length, quite forgetting to say 'sir'. He took a step into the little room, which brought him within inches of her. There was no space for her to step backwards; she couldn't very well push him aside. She stayed where she was.

'I want you to remember me.' He caught her by the shoulders and kissed her squarely on the mouth, and before she could think of anything to say he was at the door again, had opened it, and turned to say 'Tot ziens, Maggy.' He sounded as though he was laughing. She went on standing there; her sensible, orderly mind a chaotic whirl of half-formed thoughts, most which she found bewildering and disturbing, es-

pecially as she would never see him again. At length
she took off her cuffs and slowly rolled up her
sleeves, pulled on her frills, and went into the ward
to do some work.

CHAPTER TWO

FOR THE NEXT few days Maggy wasn't her usual cheerful, hard-working self. She was well aware of this, but took good care not to question herself as to the cause. She did a great deal of unnecessary work on the ward, as if the stacks of charts, laundry lists, off-duty rotas and all the other clutter accumulating on a Ward Sister's desk would make a pile sufficiently high under which to bury all thoughts of Dr Doelsma. After a time she did indeed manage to cram him into a remote corner of her mind. It was a pity that she had only just succeeded in doing this, when she was accosted by Sir Charles and asked her opinion of his erstwhile pupil. They were halfway round the ward at the time, and she had no chance to evade the question.

'He seemed a very nice wee man.' She was, idiotically, blushing.

Sir Charles gave her a look without appearing to do so.

'He's six foot four inches, Maggy, though being six foot yourself you'd not notice that. Don't you like him?'

She studied the path lab form in her hand as though she had never seen one before in her life. 'Aye. But every nurse in the hospital likes him, Sir Charles. He's a handsome man.'

Sir Charles scribbled his signature on an X-ray form before replying.

'Yes, he is. But not conceited with it. I've known him since he was a small boy—his parents were great friends of mine; his mother still is. He's clever, and he's made a successful career for himself.' He coughed. 'He knows exactly what he wants, and gets it too.' He looked so knowingly at Maggy that she went scarlet; surely Dr Doelsma hadn't told Sir Charles about the regrettable incident in her office? She realised that she hadn't forgotten it at all. Her brows drew together in so fierce a frown that Sir Charles allowed his vague manner to become even more vague, and pursued the topic in an even more ruthless fashion.

'Can't think why he's not married. Heaven knows the number of young women who have angled for him; still, as I said just now, he knows what he wants, and he has the patience to wait for it. But there, Sister, I mustn't waste your time boring on about someone you've no interest in.' He blinked rapidly and smiled disarmingly, while his elderly perceptive eye bored into hers. She met his gaze steadily.

'Aye, Sir Charles, I've no' the time to think about a man I'll not be seeing again.'

He nodded, and plunged into the highly technical details of the treatment he proposed for the patient whose bed they had reached. Mrs Salt greeted him as an old friend, gave him a colourful and most inaccurate account of her condition and asked what he'd done with the foreign doctor he'd had with him on his last visit.

'Nice, 'e was,' she reminisced. 'Now there's a man any girl could fall for.' She turned to peer at Maggy. ''Ere's one 'ose just right for 'im, too, eh?' She cackled with mischievous mirth. 'Pity 'e ain't coming again—leastways, not until me birthday—that's if yer don't let me slip through yer fingers first.'

The remark was greeted with the derision she expected, and with a brief appeal from Sister MacFergus to be good, they left her bed, and passed on to her neighbour. This was a Belgian woman, Madame Riveau, she had been admitted ten days or so before with a suspected gastric ulcer. She was a silent morose woman who only answered Maggy's basic schoolgirl French when it was absolutely necessary. She was visited regularly by her husband and her son, two equally sour and dour men, who demanded at each visit that Madame Riveau should be sent home. So far Maggy had persuaded them to let her stay, but their demands were becoming so persistent that she realised that they would soon have their way—after all, no patient could be forced to remain against their wish, although she had noticed that the woman did not seem to share her menfolk's desire for her discharge—Maggy thought she seemed frightened of them; indeed, they gave her herself an uneasy feeling of menace, which was heightened by their secretiveness when asked even the simplest of questions.

She stood looking at Madame Riveau now as Sir

Charles bent over the bed to examine her. She looked ill, and surely her face was swollen? Maggy waited until Sir Charles had finished and was conferring with his houseman before she asked in her rather halting French,

'Have you got the toothache, Madame Riveau?'

The result was electrifying. The sallow face on the pillow took on the greenish white of fear; the hate and terror in the dull black eyes sent Maggy back a pace.

'No. no! There's nothing wrong.' The woman's voice was a harsh whisper.

'There must be something wrong.' Maggy spoke gently; the woman was so obviously terrified—of the dentist perhaps? 'Supposing we get you X-rayed just to make sure before you go home?'

She was rewarded by another look of venom. 'I refuse. My teeth are sound.'

Maggy ignored the look. 'I'll talk to your husband when he comes this evening; perhaps he can persuade you.'

Sir Charles had moved on, but stopped and listened to what Maggy had to say. When she had finished he nodded, and said,

'Dr Payne can sign an X-ray form, Sister. Probably she'll be better without her teeth—she's an unhealthy woman and I should suppose she'll need surgical treatment for that ulcer...'

They became immersed in the diabetic coma in the next bed, and in the ensuing calculations of insulin units, blood sugar tests, urine tests and a great many instructions concerning the intravenous drip, Madame Riveau's strange behaviour was forgotten, and when much later Maggy remembered it, she decided she must have imagined the woman's fear and anger.

She was due off duty at six o'clock. She gave the report to Staff Nurse and then waited for the visitors to arrive. She had two days off, and she wanted to see Monsieur Riveau, and get the question of his wife's teeth settled. She felt the usual thrill of distaste as she approached the bed. The two men were seated on either side of it; neither got up as she approached, but watched her with thinly veiled hostility. She wasted no time, but explained her errand and stood waiting for a reply. The men looked at her without speaking, their faces expressionless, and yet she had a prickle of fear so real that she put her hand up to the back of her neck to brush it away. At length the elder man said, 'No X-ray, no dentist for my wife. She refuses.'

'There's no pain involved,' Maggy replied doggedly. 'Her jaws are swollen; her teeth may be infected and it may make the ulcer worse.' He said 'No' in an ugly voice, and she damped down her temper and persevered in a reasonable way, struggling with her French.

'The teeth are probably decayed; she will be better without them.' She managed to smile at the unfriendly faces. 'It's very likely that in time they will make her condition worse.'

Their silence was worse than speech—chilling and unfriendly and completely uncooperative. She could feel their dislike of her pressing against her like a tangible thing. She gave herself a mental shake, asked them to reconsider their decision, and said goodnight. Her words fell into silence like stones, and as she walked away, she could feel their eyes on her back; it was a most unpleasant sensation.

Maggy spent her two days off with a former nurse who had trained with her and then left to get married. She came back to St Ethelburga's refreshed in mind if not in body, and with a strong desire to get married and have a husband and children of her own. She thought this unlikely. She had never met a man she wished to marry; but as if to give the lie to these thoughts, a picture of Dr Doelsma, very clear and accurate down to the last detail, came into her mind's eye. She shook her head, reducing his image to fragments and said something in the Gaelic tongue with such force that Sister Beecham, sitting opposite her in the sitting room, put down her knitting and looked at her.

'I don't know what it meant, Maggy MacFergus, but it sounded as though it was a good thing I didn't, and if you are going to make the tea—I'll not have milk; I'm dieting.'

Maggy got up obediently. Sister Beecham had been at St Ethelburga's for so long that her word was law to any Sister under forty, and Maggy was only twenty-four.

As she crossed the landing the next morning, she sensed an air of suppressed excitement, although there was no one to be seen. Staff was waiting for her in her office, standing by the well-polished desk, adorned by a vase of flowers. Funeral flowers, delivered at regular intervals to the wards and hailed as a mixed blessing by the unfortunate junior nurse whose lot it was to disentangle them from their wire supports and turn the anchors and wreaths into vases of normal-looking flowers. Maggy noted with relief that Nurse had achieved a very normal-looking bunch. She detested them, but had never had the heart to say so; she guessed that some nurse had taken a lot of trouble to please her. She exchanged good mornings with Staff Nurse Williams, and thought for the hundredth time what a pretty creature she was—small and blonde and blue-eyed—everything Maggy was not and wished to be. She had discovered long ago that there were few advantages in being six feet tall. It was, for a start, impossible to be fragile or clinging; it was taken for granted that she would undertake tasks that smaller women could be helpless about, and there was always the problem of dancing partners.

Staff's eyes were sparkling; she appeared to be labouring under some emotion. Maggy sat down, saying nothing. Whatever it was could come after the report. It took fifteen minutes or so, each patient discussed treatment checked, notes made. She came to the end of the page in the report book, and, she thought, the end of the report, but Staff said in a voice of suppressed excitement, 'There's another patient, Sister. Over the page—She's a Private; in Sep.'

Maggy turned the page and the name leapt out at her. Mevrouw Van Beijen Doelsma: Coronary thrombosis. Her heart gave a lurch, but she turned no more than a faintly interested face to Williams.

'Sister, it's Dr Doelsma's mother—she's over here on holiday with Sir Charles.' Maggy nodded, remembering her conversation with him a few days ago. 'And he's been over to see her. He flew over...'

Maggy interrupted her firmly. 'When did the patient come in? Is she being specialled?'

'During the first night of your days off, Sister, and she's being specialled, though they're very short of nurses. Dr Doelsma...'

'How bad?' asked Maggy, forestalling what she felt sure was going to be a rhapsody with Dr Doelsma as the main theme.

Williams returned obediently to her report.

'Not too bad, Sister, and beginning to improve.' She went on to give a detailed account of treatment, drugs and nursing care, for she was devoted to Sister MacFergus, who was strict, kind, fair to the nurses, and had never been known to shirk the day's work; indeed, she could, if called upon, work for two—something she in fact frequently did. Williams finished her report; she had given it exactly as Sister liked it, and she hoped she was going to be asked about Dr Doelsma.

Maggy waved a capable well-kept hand at the chair. 'Sit down, Staff. Spare me two minutes and tell me all about it.'

Williams drew a long breath. 'Oh, Sister, he's smashing! He came ever so early, about eight o'clock—he flew over and stayed all day, and Sir

Charles was here, of course, and they were in there hours, I was with them. He's got a gorgeous smile, and he's so tall. He went back last night. What a pity you missed him, Sister.'

Maggy smiled. 'It sounds to me, Staff, as if he had all the help and attention he needed, I suppose you're the most envied girl in the hospital?'

Williams nodded with satisfaction. 'Yes, everyone's green with envy.' She gazed out of the window. 'He wore the loveliest waistcoat,' she said.

Maggy got up, telling herself that she had not the least desire to discuss the doctor's waistcoats. 'Williams, what about your faithful Jim?'

The other girl sighed. 'I know, Sister, but Dr Doelsma's like someone out of a dream—the sort of man you always want to meet, and never do. If he comes again, Sister, you'll see what I mean.'

Maggy saw exactly what she meant. 'I'm going to do my round,' she said firmly. She went to Sep last. Mevrouw Doelsma looked very small lying there in bed. Despite her grey pallor, Maggy could see that she was a most attractive woman, with white hair, excellently cut. Her eyes were closed, and Maggy stood with the charts, studying them, and listening to the nurse's report. Everything looked satisfactory. She sent the nurse to go and get her coffee, and turned back to the bed. Her patient's eyes were open and upon her. She smiled, but before she could say anything, Mevrouw Doelsma spoke.

'Maggy? I'm so glad. Charles said you would get me well.'

'Yes, of course, Mevrouw Doelsma, we'll have you well again very soon.'

The little lady smiled. 'Paul was cross because you weren't here. He had to go back.'

A faint colour stole into Maggy's cheeks at the mention of his name, but she told herself that he was probably annoyed because the Ward Sister wasn't on duty night and day. There were quite a few doctors who regarded nurses as machines who could work twenty-four hours a day. The door opened and Sir Charles Warren came in. He nodded in the direction of the bed and said. 'Hullo, Henrietta.' Then he turned to Maggy. 'There you are. Pity you weren't here when Mevrouw Doelsma came in. Nice little staff nurse you've got; you've trained her well, but she's not a patch on you. Still, you're here now. I'll have a look at the patient and we'll do an ECG and then we can have a chat.'

Half an hour later he followed Maggy into her office, accepted a cup of coffee, drank it scalding hot and demanded another. Maggy poured it out and put in his usual four lumps of sugar.

'You'll get an ulcer, Sir Charles,' she said severely.

He agreed comfortably. 'Now, Mevrouw Doelsma. She should do. I think. Had a nasty coronary, but it seems to be settling. There's always the chance of another one, though. Let me know at once, Maggy. You know what to do until I arrive.' He got to his feet. 'I must go.' He gave a friendly smile, and made for the door which Maggy was holding open for him. 'Glad it's you looking after her, Sister. Couldn't wish for anyone better. If anyone pulls her through it'll be you.' He nodded in a satisfied way and went.

The rest of the day was busy. Maggy found to her annoyance that Madame Riveau had still refused to have her X-rays. She would have liked to have seen her husband during the evening visiting hours, but there was no nurse available for specialling after six o'clock, so she left Staff in charge of the ward, and went into Sep herself. It was ten o'clock before she could be relieved by a night nurse.

Mevrouw Doelsma was an excellent patient, and had gone quietly to sleep. Maggy thought she had a good chance of recovery.

Williams wasn't on duty until one o'clock, so that Maggy had a very busy morning. She was glad to go off duty after dinner, although she knew she would have to come back early. There was a nurse off sick, and extra beds up and down the centre of the ward. But she didn't mind hard work. The ward was straight by seven o'clock, and she sent Williams and a junior nurse to supper. It was visiting time; the patients were occupied with their visitors. Maggy sat in Sep with the door open, so that she could see down the ward, and watch Mevrouw Doelsma at the same time; she was awake and lying quietly.

The restlessness came on suddenly. Maggy put down the report book and got to the bed as Mevrouw Doelsma gave a couple of painful gasps, went livid, and lapsed into unconsciousness. Maggy turned on the oxygen, and strapped the nasal catheter in position, then drew up and gave an injection of morphia. Only then did she press the button which would turn on the red light above the door of Sep. There was little hope of a nurse back from supper; there was a full five minutes to go, but someone might see it and come to investigate. She could feel no pulse under her steady fingers; she adjusted the BP armband on the flaccid arm, but could get no sound through the stethoscope; with it still swinging around her neck, she turned to draw the heparin and mephine.

She knew exactly what to do, and did it with calm speed, reflecting that it would have been easier with two. She had the syringe in hand when Dr Doelsma walked in. Without a word she handed it to him, and held the limp arm rigid so that he could inject the blood vessel in the elbow. 'Heparin,' she said. 'I gave morphia'—she glanced at the clock—'two minutes ago. The mephine is drawn up.'

He nodded, jabbed the needle in, took the mephine from her and gave that too.

She gave him the stethoscope and said quietly, 'I'll ring Sir Charles.' She sent her urgent message, and went back to find the doctor sitting on the edge of the bed, his mother's hand in his.

Mevrouw Doelsma still looked very ill, but they could see now that she wasn't going to die. Maggy wrote up the charts; Sir Charles would expect them accurate and ready for him. Dr Doelsma was using the stethoscope again; he took it off and handed it to Maggy. This time it recorded something—a poor something, but obviously the drugs were having effect. They agreed their reading, and smiled at each other; she could see how anxious his eyes were. They both stood looking down at the face on the pillow between them. It held some semblance of life again, and as they watched, the eyelids fluttered and his mother's eyes opened. She looked at her son and then at Maggy, and a tiny smile came and went, but as she was about to speak he gave her hand a warning squeeze.

'Don't talk, Mama, everything's all right. You shall have your say presently.'

She smiled again before she closed her eyes again. They stood on either side of her, patiently waiting. There was nothing very much to do now, except regular and frequent pulse and BP checks. By the time Sir Charles arrived, it was normal. He looked at the charts while he listened to Maggy's concise, brief report. He nodded at Dr Doelsma. 'Not much for me to do, eh, Paul? Lucky you turned up when you did.' He spent a little time examining his patient and said, 'She'll do, thanks to you, Paul.'

The other man shook his head. 'It is Sister MacFergus whom we must both thank. She did everything necessary in the most competent manner.'

Sir Charles smiled at Maggy. 'Yes, she always does. A most reliable girl.'

The two men stood looking at her; it was a relief to find Staff Nurse at her elbow.

'Shall I clear up here, Sister? Nurse Sims has got the ward straight—the night staff are on.'

Maggy thought a minute. 'Nurse Sims can go now;

I'll give the report, then you can go. I'll stay here until they can send another nurse.'

Williams said eagerly, 'I'll stay...' but was interrupted by Sir Charles.

'Will you stay here for a while, Sister? Have you a good nurse for night duty here?'

Maggy shook her head. 'There's a shortage of nurses, Sir Charles, it's this gastric bug. There's no nurse at present, but Matron will arrange for one later on, I'm sure. I'll bide till she comes.' She looked at Williams and saw the disappointment on her face. 'When I come back, Staff, will you make coffee for all of us. I'm sure the doctors would like a cup.' She was rewarded by a grateful smile as she turned to Sir Charles.

'I'll give the report, sir, and be back. Staff Nurse will clear up and set the room ready.' She gave Williams the keys and slipped away, watched by the two doctors.

Paul said low-voiced, 'When Mother goes back home to Oudehof, I want Sister MacFergus to go with her.'

Sir Charles pursed his lips and looked doubtfully at his companion, who met his gaze with a cool determined look of his own.

'She's a ward sister, you know.'

'I know. Could she not have special leave for a couple of weeks or so? I'll pay whatever fee the hospital requires. I want someone I can trust to look after Mother.'

'Naturally. And you trust Sister MacFergus?'

'Yes, Uncle Charles, I do.'

The older man turned away and bent over his patient. There was a faint pink in her cheeks now; her pulse was regular and much stronger. He gave Williams some instructions, and went back to Paul. 'Very well, Paul, I'll do my best for you. Your mother will be here for a month—you know that. I daresay something can be arranged in the meantime. But I think we will say nothing of this for the time being. Do you agree?'

Paul nodded. 'I'd like to stay the night. I don't need to be back in Leiden until Monday morning.'

He broke off as Maggy came back into the room. She nodded to Williams, then took off her cuffs and rolled up her sleeves.

'Staff's making coffee. You'll have a cup, Sir Charles? And you, sir? It'll be ready in my office.'

'And you, Sister?' It was Dr Doelsma speaking.

'I'll be here, sir. I'll have mine later.' She didn't even look at him, but busied herself with the drip.

Williams was waiting for them, hovering over Sister's own coffee pot, very anxious to please. There were only two chairs, so Dr Doelsma sat on the desk and drank his coffee.

'Are you not off duty, Staff Nurse?'

Williams, the faithful Jim's image temporarily dimmed, fluttered her eyelashes and used a dimple devastatingly.

'Yes, sir. But the night staff haven't time to make coffee now.'

'And Sister?'

'She's off too. Oh...' she remembered... 'she's not been to supper, and she'll be on duty until two o'clock—there's no one to take over before then. I must make her some sandwiches.' She forgot all about charming the Dutch doctor in her anxiety for Sister MacFergus.

'Sister is fortunate to have a staff nurse who takes such care of her.' He smiled down at the pretty little creature. Something in his face made her realise suddenly that behind his rather arrogant good looks there was strength of character, as well as kindness and a concern for others; it became of paramount importance to her to win his good opinion.

'No, we're the lucky ones. I mean the nurses on this ward. You see, sir, Sister's one of the nicest people any of us have ever met. Of course, we all call her Maggy behind her back, but that's because we like her—' She broke off and looked uncertainly at Sir Charles who called Sister MacFergus Maggy to her face.

'A good Scottish name,' he murmured, and got up. With a smile and a nod of thanks he went back to Sep where the ECG machine was ready by the bed. He said, 'Right, Sister,' and Maggy started fastening the straps very carefully and gently, leaving Dr Doelsma to connect up the leads, and then stood back, waiting for the doctors to make a recording. They had just finished when Williams came in, whispered to her, said a low goodnight, and went off duty. Maggy had hardly begun to disconnect the leads before Dr Doelsma was by her side.

'I'll do that, Sister. Go and have your coffee and sandwiches.' She glanced at Sir Charles. 'Yes, Maggy, go and sit down for ten minutes. I'll be over presently before I go. Dr Doelsma will be staying the night; he'll be on hand if you want anyone in a hurry.'

The night passed slowly. There wasn't a great deal to do. The doctor had refused the offer of a bed in the housemen's quarters, but had remained in the room, sitting relaxed and calm in an easy chair near the bed. He had opened the dispatch case he had brought with him, and was busily engaged writing. Maggy supposed it was another lecture.

Just after midnight Mevrouw Doelsma woke up, asked for water in a thin voice and wanted to know the time. Maggy told her, and she frowned and whispered, 'You poor child, you must be worn out; you've been here all day.'

Maggy hastened to assure her that she wasn't in the least tired, but her patient only smiled and said, 'Stuff!' and then. 'But I'm glad you were here. I felt quite safe with you.' She turned her head to look at her son, standing beside her, his fingers on her pulse. 'I won't do it again. Don't go just yet, will you?'

'I can stay until tomorrow night, dear; you'll be feeling much better by then.' He gave the hand a squeeze and smiled, and she closed her eyes again, saying, 'You're both so enormous.'

Just before two o'clock, Maggy's relief arrived. She was a senior student and a very good nurse, and a very attractive one too. Maggy introduced the doctor, gave a report, said goodnight, and made for the door. The doctor, with the advantage of longer legs, got there first, opened it, and then filled the doorway with his bulk so that it was impossible for her to go through.

'I'm in your debt, Sister MacFergus,' he looked steadily into her weary face. 'You saved my mother's life. You have my gratitude and my thanks.'

'And I'll thank ye also, Doctor, for if ye hadna' come when ye did, I ken fine it might have gone ill with your mother.' She smiled, all six feet of her drooping with tiredness. 'Goodnight, sir.' She slipped past him and was gone.

Maggy was quite her usual self when she went on duty the next morning. She took the report and then went into Sep, Dr Doelsma rose from his chair and wished her a good morning. He looked immaculate, freshly shaven, and not a crease to be seen; his face was that of a man who had enjoyed an untroubled night's rest. The patient was sleeping, and according to the night nurse, entirely satisfactory. She picked up her report ready to give it, and was about to begin when Dr Doelsma coughed gently. 'Er—shall I go, Sister, or may I stay?' He sounded so meek that she shot him a suspicious glance before asking him politely to do as he wished. He settled back into his chair which creaked alarmingly under his weight, and opened out *The Times,* only lowering it briefly to wish the night nurse a warm farewell, coupled with a solicitous wish that she would sleep soundly, and all without a glance at Maggy, who had not failed to notice with an unusual flash of temper that he and the night nurse appeared to be on excellent terms. Despite herself, she gave an angry snort,

He lowered *The Times* for a second time. 'You spoke, Sister?'

'I did not,' she snapped, and added 'sir.'

He folded his paper carefully, glanced at his sleeping parent and asked.

'Must I be called sir?'

She charted the pulse carefully.

'Of course, Dr Doelsma. You are a consultant.'

'So, by the same token, I may call you Maggy?'

She took a deep breath and said deliberately, 'You are in a position to call me anything you wish, sir.' She realised her mistake as soon as she had spoken.

'My dear girl, how kind of you.' His voice was smooth. 'I wonder, what shall it be?'

She blushed under his mocking eye, and said with dignity, 'That's not what I meant, Doctor, and you know it.' She put down the chart and went on briskly, 'I doubt you'll be wanting your breakfast—I'll arrange that.'

'Don't bother—er—Sister. Now that you're here, I'll go over and see Sir Charles and breakfast with him. I'll be back within the hour.'

'Very well, sir, I'll ring you if it should be necessary.'

She ignored him, and prepared to take Mevrouw Doelsma's blood pressure. Her patient opened her eyes at that moment, and said, 'Hullo, it's you again.

I'm glad. A sweet girl, the night nurse, but so earnest, I felt as though I had one foot in the grave all night.'

Maggy smiled and said gently. 'Fiddlesticks, you were dreaming—and both feet are safe here in bed.'

She turned to find Dr Doelsma still there, looming over the end of the bed.

He said, 'Hullo, Mama. I'm going over to Uncle Charles. Be good.' He turned at the door, with his hand on the knob.

'You'll ring me, won't you, Sister?' He sounded casual, but she could see the worry in his eyes.

She smiled at him warmly. 'Of course.' She looked supremely confident and capable, standing there in her trim uniform.

There was still a shortage of nurses; if Williams was to get her half day. Maggy thought, she herself would have to go off duty that morning. She decided to do so as soon as Dr Doelsma returned. Williams could look after the ward, and Sibley, the third-year nurse, could come into Sep. Sir Charles came back with Dr Doelsma, they looked well fed and relaxed. Maggy, who had had a sketchy breakfast, thought longingly of coffee... She would never get off duty by ten o'clock. It was a quarter past the hour when Sir Charles finished examining his patient. He held a short discussion with Paul and called for another ECG.

Maggy was buckling the straps when Dr Doelsma came over to do his part.

'Are you not off duty, Sister?' She glanced up in surprise.

'How did you know?'

'That pretty little staff nurse of yours told me. Shall I get her in so that you can go?'

She tightened a buckle slowly. 'Why not?' she asked coolly. 'Though I'm afraid Staff won't be able to come for long. But Nurse Sibley shall relieve her; she's the pretty blonde with green eyes—I'm sure you will have noticed her.'

She didn't look up to see what effect her words had had, but finished what she was doing, sent for Williams to take her place, and went to the ward. By the time she had done a round it was almost eleven. She decided to have coffee in the Sisters' Home, but when she got there it didn't seem worth while. Dinner would be at twelve-thirty. She flounced into the sitting room, feeling pettish and more than a little sorry for herself, and buried herself in the papers for the next hour or so. There weren't any other Sisters off; she wished she had not bothered to go off duty at all, though that, she decided, would not have pleased Dr Doelsma, for then he would have had to have put up with her for the whole morning.

She returned on duty after lunch, her frame of mind by no means improved. The ward was fairly quiet. She sent Nurse Sibley to her dinner, and Williams to her afternoon with the faithful Jim. That left little Nurse Sims whom she sent into the ward to tidy it for visitors; she herself went into Sep until Sibley should return. Both doctors had gone to lunch; her patient was sleeping. She studied the charts and then started to pick up the papers littered around the doctor's chair. They were closely written in a foreign language—Dutch, she supposed; in any case, they would have been unintelligible in English. She made a tidy pile, then went to open the window wider. It was a lovely late August day; she would have liked to have been home, tramping the hills with the dogs. The door opened, but she didn't turn round at once, but said,

'You should have taken your full hour, Nurse; I'll not need to go until two o'clock.'

She looked over her shoulder. Dr Doelsma was standing in the doorway.

'You're at lunch,' she said stupidly.

He ignored this piece of foolishness, but strolled into the room.

'Ah. I'm glad you're back on duty,' he said.

She frowned. Really, she thought, after his obvious anxiety to get rid of her that morning—'Did something go wrong?' she asked.

'No, no. Nurse Sibley was most competent, but I must admit that I prefer you here, Sister.' He stared at her. 'You needed to go off duty this morning, you were tired.'

She went pink; it was an unpleasant experience having her thoughts read so accurately. She asked, curiosity getting the better of discretion, 'Why do you prefer me here, Doctor?'

He considered his reply. 'I am a big man, Sister. People tend to stare at me as though I were something peculiar. You don't stare, presumably because you are such a big woman yourself. A purely selfish reason, you see.'

This truthful but unflattering description of herself did nothing to improve Maggy's mood, and the more so because she could think of nothing to say in reply. Nurse Sibley's return saved her from this difficulty, however. She handed over to her, and left the room with great dignity, feeling twelve feet tall, and very conscious of the largeness of her person.

The visitors, laden with flowers and fruit and unsuitable food, began to straggle in, and Maggy was kept busy answering questions and making out certificates. Madame Riveau's husband and son hadn't arrived; she would have to see them that evening. She sat down at her desk and began the off-duty rota for the following week. It was an absorbing and irritating task, trying to fit in lectures, study days, and special requests for days off. She became immersed in it, then looked up to find the doctor standing by her. She stopped, pen poised.

'Did you want me, sir?'

He didn't answer her question, but said shortly, 'My mother's asleep.' He stretched out an arm and took the off duty book from her and studied it carefully. Maggy asked in an annoyed voice,

'Is there something you wish to know, Dr Doelsma?'

'Yes, there was,' he answered cheerfully, 'but I've seen all I want, thank you.' He gave the book back into a hand rendered nerveless with vexation, but made no effort to go.

Maggy filled in another name and then asked, 'Would you like tea, sir? It's early, I know, but perhaps in Holland you drink tea at a different time from us.'

'Probably. But I must point out to you that I am a Friesman, and not a Hollander, and proud of the fact—just as you, I imagine, are proud of being a Scotswoman. The Friesians and the Scots have mutual ancestors, you know.'

Maggy didn't know, and said so, adding, 'How interesting' in a cold voice which he ignored.

'How's Mrs Salt?' he enquired.

Maggy put down her pen in a deliberate manner. He seemed bent on engaging her in conversation, however unwilling on her part, so she said civilly, 'The path lab results came back yesterday—and the X-rays show an infiltration into the oesophagus—a blueprint of your lecture.'

'May I see her notes?' He was serious and rather remote now. She got the notes and X-rays and answered his questions sensibly. At length he handed them back to her, saying, 'A blueprint indeed, Sister, which bears out your question, does it not?'

She nodded. 'It's strange that a condition as rare as this one should coincide with your lecture.'

They discussed technicalities for a few minutes, and she surprised him with her sharp brain and knowledge used with so much intelligence.

'Could you spare time to come and see Mrs Salt?' he suggested. 'Not to examine her, just a social visit.'

They walked down the ward to the old lady's bed.

She had no visitors—she had been a patient for so long that the novelty of coming to see her had worn off—and she hailed Dr Doelsma with delight.

'Cor, if it ain't Dr Dutch 'isself!' She extended a hand, which he observed had become more transparent, and if possible thinner than it had been a week ago. Her lively black eyes snapped at him, however.

'Don't feed me a lot of codswallop about getting better, doctor. I ain't a fool, no more I'm a cry-baby, though I'll be fair mad if I don't 'ave me birthday.' She turned her penetrating gaze on to Maggy. 'Goin' to 'ave a cake, ain't I, love?'

Sister MacFergus, replying to this endearing form of address, smiled and said, 'Yes, Mrs Salt, a cake with candles, so you'd better be good and do as you're asked so that you'll be able to blow them out. There'll be presents too.' she added.

The old lady brightened. ''Oo from?'

Maggy smiled. 'That's a secret, but I can promise that you're going to get quite a lot of parcels.'

'Suppose I don't last, love?'

Maggy didn't hesitate. 'Mrs Salt, I promise you that you shall have a birthday party.'

The old lady nodded, satisfied. 'Right yer are. You're coming, young man?' She turned briskly to the doctor.

His eyes widened with laughter. 'No one's called me young man for years! How nice it sounds. For that I shall bring you a birthday present. Will you choose, or shall it be a surprise?'

'I'll 'ave a pink nightie with lots of lace,' she replied promptly. 'It'll cost yer a pretty penny; d'yer earn enough to buy one?'

He didn't smile, but answered gently, 'Yes, Mrs Salt, I do, and you shall have it—on condition that you wear it at the party.'

'O' course I shall! A bit of a waste on an old woman like me, ain't it? but I always wanted one—more sense ter give it ter Sister 'ere. She'd look nice in it, I reckon.'

Maggy kept her eyes on the counterpane, and concentrated on not blushing, but was well aware that Dr Doelsma was studying her with interest and taking his time about it.

'Yes, very nice, Mrs Salt,' he murmured, 'but she'll have to wait for her birthday, won't she?'

He said goodbye then, and they turned away. Madame Riveau, in the next bed, had visitors. Her husband and son sat one on each side of her; they looked, Maggy thought, as though they were guarding the woman in the bed. She wished them a good afternoon as she passed, and was surprised when they both got up and walked over to her. Subconsciously she recoiled and took an instinctive step towards the doctor, who looked faintly surprised but remained silent.

The older man spoke. 'I wish to take my wife home. You will arrange it?' It wasn't a request but a demand, couched in an insolent tone and awkward French.

Maggy stopped. 'I'm sorry, Monsieur Riveau; you must arrange that with the doctor. Your wife is almost better; please let her stay for another week.'

The younger man had joined his father. 'My mother is not to have her teeth X-rayed or drawn.' There was an ill-concealed dislike in his voice.

Maggy glanced at him briefly, refusing to be intimidated. Dr Doelsma had remained silent, but his presence gave her a good deal of courage.

'Your mother is in pain; surely she may decide herself?'

His small black eyes glared at her. She couldn't understand what he said, but evidently the doctor could. He stopped him and began to speak in a voice Maggy hadn't heard him use before; it was cold and hard and full of authority. He spoke in fluent French which she couldn't hope to follow, and she watched the two men cringe under it. When the doctor had finished, they made no reply but looked at Maggy with hate in their eyes, and went back to the bed.

Maggy stood irresolute, but Dr Doelsma tapped her on the shoulder in a peremptory fashion, and she found herself, rather to her own surprise, walking meekly beside him down the ward. By the time they had reached her office, however, she had begun to feel a slight indignation. He had had no right to interfere when she was discussing her own patients; the fact that she had been very glad to have him there while he talked with those two awful men had nothing to do with it. Standing by her desk, she said stiffly,

'Thank you for your help, although I am usually judged capable of dealing with matters concerning my patients.'

She was vexed to hear her voice shaking. She was enraged still further when he laughed.

'How pretty you are when you are angry! I'm sorry you are annoyed with me. Was I very high-handed? You didn't understand what that man was saying, did you? Shall I tell you, or will you take my word for it that he was crude and disgusting? If we had been anywhere else but a hospital ward, I should have knocked him down.'

She looked startled and contrite. 'I didn't understand him, you were kind to…to stop him. Thank you.'

'Why are you afraid of them?'

'Oh! How did you know—did they see…?'

'No, they did not. I don't blame you for disliking them. I found them most repulsive.' He smiled. 'Am I forgiven?'

'Yes, of course, sir. I'm sorry I was rude.' She looked at him anxiously. He was still smiling—she remembered that he had smiled on the day of the lecture and said quickly in a brisk fashion, 'Now I'll be helping Nurse with the teas. The visitors will be going…' She got as far as the door.

'My mother complains bitterly that she has hardly seen you all day. Could not the green-eyed blonde help with teas while you come into Sep? She has proved a poor substitute for you, Sister.'

She bristled. 'Nurse Sibley is a very competent nurse.'

Their eyes met; his were dancing with laughter.

'Indeed yes, Maggy. But that isn't what I meant.'

She found she had been ushered out of the office and across the landing into Sep and heard herself telling Nurse Sibley to go the ward and help with teas. She seemed to be doing exactly what the doctor wished her to do. She remembered Sir Charles' words, and made a resolve to be very much firmer in the future.

CHAPTER THREE

DR DOELSMA went back to Holland during Sunday night, and the ward seemed a very dull place without him. Maggy felt a thrill of excitement when Sir Charles mentioned in a casual manner that Paul would be visiting his mother at the end of the week. Nevertheless she felt constrained to change her off-duty so that she would be absent from the ward on that day. Staff Nurse Williams looked at her as if she was out of her mind.

'Sister! Dr Doelsma's coming—he'll get here about two o'clock and he's going again in the evening. You'll miss him.'

'Well, that can't be helped,' said Maggy reasonably. 'I promised I would go and see this friend of my mother's and it just so happens that she wants me to go on Friday.' She smiled at Williams. 'You can cope with anything that may crop up, and Mevrouw Doelsma is so much better now, I think she'll do. Besides, Dr Doelsma thinks you're a very pretty girl, and you know you're delighted to be seeing him.'

Williams giggled, 'Well, Sister, he is marvellous!'

So Maggy spent her day with elderly Miss Mac-Intyre, who hadn't seen her for a number of years and treated her like a schoolgirl; they went for a walk in the park, and changed the library books and discussed

49

knitting patterns, and she went back to the hospital in the evening, wondering if she would be like Miss MacIntyre in forty years' time.

Rather to her surprise, the next morning, Williams gave her the report without mentioning Dr Doelsma, but as Maggy closed the report book her staff nurse opened a cupboard and produced an opulent box of Kersenbonbons, and laid it on the desk.

'He brought these,' she breathed. 'I said you weren't here, and he said how nice it was to see me again, and he gave me these and I told him I'd give them to you, and he said No, they're for the nurses, Sister will get something next time I come—but we thought we'd save them for you all the same.'

A small lump of hurt feelings settled in Maggy's throat, but she swallowed it resolutely.

'That was sweet of you all, but you take them and divide them up amongst you—Dr Doelsma might feel hurt in his feelings if ye didna' do as he asked.' She got up from her chair. 'Sit down now, Staff, and do it this minute.' She smiled at the other girl. 'I'm off on my round.'

As she went she told herself that it was her own fault anyway that she hadn't been on duty. Staff had said that he was coming again on the following Sunday—it was her free weekend in any case. The thought put her in mind of the amount of work she had to do, and she resolutely put all thoughts of the doctor out of her mind.

When she got to Mrs Salt's bed, she found that old lady in a gossiping mood.

'Yer missed 'im,' she informed Maggy. 'And now it's yer weekend, ain't it, love, so yer won't see 'im then either. But I 'eard 'im asking Staff if you was on duty next Thursday evening, and she said Yes, and 'e says Good, I'll be along then. So you'll see 'im then.'

Maggy straightened a pillow. 'Is that so, Mrs Salt? And I've just remembered that I'll have to change my off duty on Thursday. Isn't that a pity?'

She turned to the next bed, and found Madame Riveau sitting up in a chair. She would be going home very soon now, but she looked ill and spiritless. Maggy eyed her swollen jaws but remained silent. It was to be hoped that the woman would go to her own dentist as soon as she got home. She asked a few questions of her, but her answers were surly and unwilling, so she left her and went on down the ward and finally into Sep.

Mevrouw Doelsma smiled at her from her pillows, and Maggy thought how pretty she was now that she was better and had some colour in her cheeks, and a faint sparkle in her eyes.

'Maggy, Paul missed you yesterday. He expected you to be on duty.' Maggy went across the room and adjusted the blind, then said, with her back to her patient,

'I changed my off-duty at the last minute.' She smiled over her shoulder.

'And you won't be here tomorrow either?'

'No, it's my weekend, but Staff is very efficient...'

Mevrouw Doelsma looked at Maggy's rather nice

back view. 'I wouldn't dream of asking you to lose a minute of your free time, but I'm selfish enough to like you here all the time. Oh well, he'll be over again on Thursday. You'll be here then, won't you?'

Maggy hesitated; she didn't like telling lies. 'Well, I usually am.' She achieved the half truth, feeling guilty.

She spent the weekend trying to think of a good excuse for changing her evening off. It was nothing short of a miracle that Williams should come to her during Monday and ask if she could possibly have Wednesday evening free. Maggy breathed a sigh of relief and, taking care not to appear too pleased, agreed.

Wednesday evening was fairly quiet. She did the medicine round and started the report before going to supper, and when she came back went to see Mevrouw Doelsma, who was sitting up in bed, ready for someone to talk to. She looked rather excited, Maggy thought, as she tidied her pillows, she supposed that she was pleased because she was making such good progress. Another two weeks and there would be talk of her going home. It was almost eight-thirty. She switched off the ceiling light, leaving the little bedside lamp burning, and went to the door and opened it, then turned round again to say,

'I'm going to give the report, Mevrouw Doelsma. Ring if you want anything; I'll be in to say goodnight later.' She stepped backwards on to a foot, and didn't need to hear the chuckle above her left ear to know whose it was. A very large gentle hand clipped her round the waist.

'And do you number me among your enemies that you trample me so ruthlessly under foot? At best a poor way of greeting me after almost two weeks!'

She stood within the circle of his arm, fighting to breathe normally.

'Ye ken well you're no enemy of mine, Dr Doelsma—and I didna' expect ye.'

He dropped his arm and she turned to face him with what dignity she could muster.

He smiled at her. 'No, you didn't, did you, Sister MacFergus? I should have warned you not to try the same trick twice.'

She opened her mouth to speak, but only succeeded in making a small choking sound.

'That's right,' he said kindly. 'I wouldn't say anything you may regret later. And if you want to know how I found out, I have no intention of telling you.' He looked down at his well brushed shoes. 'Aren't you going to say you're sorry? I'm in great pain...'

Maggy laughed, 'Oh, Dr Doelsma, what's to be done with you?'

'I'm open to suggestions,' he murmured.

Maggy frowned. 'Yes, well,' she said briskly, 'I'll away to give the report.' She smiled at Mevrouw Doelsma and swept past him without a glance.

He went over to the bed then, kissed his mother, and tumbled a pile of books on to the bed-table. 'I've been to see Uncle Charles,' he said. 'He's very satisfied, Mother. If we can get Maggy to accompany you home, I should think you could go in a fortnight. You'll have to lead a quiet life for several weeks, you know.'

He drew up a chair, and they became immersed in plans.

There was a subdued hum of voices coming from behind the shut door of the office. Maggy opened the door and stood looking around her, too surprised to speak. The night nurses as well as Sibley and Sims were there, feverishly arranging a vast number of red roses into vases. Sibley looked up when the door opened, and said. 'Sister, Dr Doelsma asked us to put them in water—he brought them for you.'

Maggy closed her mouth, which had dropped open. 'But there are dozens. They can't all be for me, there must be some mistake.'

'No, Sister. He said, ''These are all for Sister MacFergus.'' There's six dozen of them,' she added in an awed voice.

'How nice.' Maggy's voice sounded faint in her own ears. 'Thank you for arranging them.' She sent the day nurses off duty, and sitting in a bower of roses, gave the report. After she had done a round with the night nurse she went back to the office. The little room smelled delicious, she crossed the landing to Sep and went in. The doctor unfolded himself from his chair.

'I hear that my mother's progress is excellent, Sister.' He looked and sounded exactly like any other consultant—friendly, cool and remote.

She answered suitably, sedately, wished her patient

a good night and went back to the door, feeling awkward. He opened it for her, and stood back politely, waiting for her to pass through. She stopped in the doorway, and raised her eyes to his, she sounded breathless.

'The roses are beautiful, thank you, Doctor. But I think the nurses mistook your message to me. They'll be for all of us and the ward too?'

'Your nurses made no mistake, Sister. The roses are for you.'

'But there are six dozen of them, Doctor; ye canna mean to give me seventy-two roses?' She looked at him, bewildered.

'Indeed I do mean it, Sister MacFergus.'

'I've never had such a lovely bouquet in my life before,' she said naïvely. 'I love red roses.'

'I'm glad. There's some charming poetry written about red roses,' he observed.

She was very conscious of him watching her while she thought. It didn't take her long to remember. She went pink and said,

'Aye, I expect so; I don't read poetry much—no time, that is.' She was becoming incoherent.

'Oh, come,' he said easily, 'everyone learns poetry at school. What about, ''My love is like a red red rose''?'

'Well, yes, I'd—' She had been going to say that she had forgotten it; but she hadn't. 'There must be any number...such a lovely colour...and long stems...' She looked rather wildly at him.

'Maggy, you're babbling.' He was laughing at her.

She didn't know whether to laugh with him or cry; she felt unaccountably like doing both. He stopped laughing and said quite seriously,

'I want to talk to you. Will you be here next Wednesday?'

She nodded and said goodnight in a low voice, then fled through the door and over to her office, and stood amongst the roses until she heard him shut the door. Then she picked a bunch of roses from one of the vases and went over to the Sisters' Home.

Maggy lay awake a long time trying to think sensibly. But good sense had no chance against the wisps of wild dreams floating in and out of her head. She wondered what he wanted to see her about, and then caught the tatters of her common sense about her, and told herself sharply to stop behaving like a lovesick schoolgirl and go to sleep.

In the morning the first thing she saw was the bunch of roses, and she remembered what Sister Beecham had said when they had met on the way to her room the night before.

'Red Roses, MacFergus? Who's in love with you?'

'In love with me?' She must have sounded stupid, for the older woman had answered impatiently, 'Of course. You must know that men send red roses to the girls they love.' She had sniffed. 'Still, perhaps they don't do it nowadays.'

At the memory of her remark, Maggy said 'Nonsense' very loudly and got out of bed, deliberately filling her mind with thoughts as practical as the uniform she was putting on.

* * *

She had little time for private thoughts during the next few days. Mrs Salt, prostrate after a sudden bout of pain and sickness, needed a great deal of encouragement and attention if she was to survive to celebrate her birthday. It took the combined skill and cunning of the nursing staff, coupled with pep talks from Sir Charles and the house physician, to get her sitting up against her pillows again.

Maggy had another problem on her hands too—Madame Riveau, due to go home in a couple of days, looked increasingly ill. Despite this, her husband and son asked sullenly each time they came if she could leave immediately. To her surprise, Madame Riveau had consented to have her teeth X-rayed on the morning of her discharge, but Maggy guessed that she had not told either her husband or her son. If she could persuade them to wait until the day the doctor had agreed upon for her discharge she could be seen before they called to fetch her home. The woman had been a lot of trouble and she would be glad to see her go.

Wednesday came at last. When she went into Sep, Maggy was greeted by Mevrouw Doelsma, whose manner was faintly tinged with excitement, but she chatted guilelessly while Maggy helped her out of her armchair and back into bed. When she was once more sitting back comfortably against the pillows she gave a contented sigh.

'It's wonderful to get up each day now, but bed is

so delightful afterwards. I'm doing well, aren't I, Maggy?'

She was answered by a muffled voice from under her bed, where Maggy was lying, plugging in a second lamp. Sep, as Maggy had so often said, had been designed by a man with no imagination. The wall plugs were all ground level, behind the bed, and the nurses had long ago discovered that it was both quick and easy to reach them by getting under the bed rather than to pull the bed out from the wall, and then push it back again. Mrs Doelsma, having seen this operation performed countless times, thought nothing of the shapely pair of legs sticking out from under the side of her bed, but continued to address them.

'Do you suppose I shall be able to go home soon? I've been very happy here, but now I feel almost well again, and I should like to go back to Oudehof.'

Her voice tailed off. Her son was standing in the doorway; he gave a half smile in greeting and raised an eyebrow at the legs, but made no attempt to come into the room. There was a click, as the lamp was switched on.

'Of course you'll be going home soon, Mevrouw Doelsma.' Maggy spoke in a comforting voice. She had heard the slightly wistful note in the little lady's voice. She slid from under the bed and stood up. For all her size, she was a very graceful young woman; she gave herself a shake, twitched her apron bib straight, smiled at Mevrouw Doelsma, and turned in a leisurely fashion to the door. The sight of the doctor brought her up short. She blushed, to her own annoyance, and said in a rather weak voice. 'Oh! Have you been there long?' She looked at him anxiously, but there was nothing to read from his face. Perhaps he had just that minute arrived.

He smiled briefly and said, 'I'm early, I believe, Sister. I hope it is not inconvenient?' He sounded brisk and rather aloof. Just as though, thought Maggy, he had never seen red roses in his life. Well, she could be brisk too.

'No, sir, it's not inconvenient. Mevrouw Doelsma is quite ready to see you.'

She smiled at her patient and slipped through the door, determined to be very busy in the ward for the rest of the day; there were only a couple of hours to go before the night staff came on. She did the medicine round, and was writing her report at her desk when the doctor knocked and came in.

He spoke without preamble. 'Will you spare me five minutes of your time—there is something I want to ask you.' He pulled up a chair and sat down and smiled at her to make her heart turn over.

'Mother will be going home to Friesland in ten days or so.' He paused. 'Maggy, I'm not giving you much time to make up your mind about this—I want you to come too.' His voice was urgent.

Maggy, sitting very upright with her hands folded on her apron, kept her eyes on the desk. She was deafened by the thudding of her heart; her mind a jumble of thoughts and dreams. Before she had time to reply he went on,

'It will be just for a few weeks; you're an excellent

nurse, and my mother is fond of you. I can trust her to your care, I know. I must confess that we thought of this some time ago, but I was doubtful if you would come.'

He sat back, looking at her smilingly. Maggy smiled back, pride keeping her mouth steady and her eyes dry. There would be plenty of time later on to call herself the silly romantic fool she undoubtedly was. She thought fleetingly of the red roses—all part of the softening process perhaps, deliberately planned so that she would fall in with his suggestion? When she spoke, her voice was quite steady.

'I'm flattered by your good opinion of me, sir, but I think that Matron will not allow it.'

He said with a trace of arrogance, 'I saw Matron some time ago about this. We—that is, Sir Charles and I—managed to persuade her to agree to you going. Provided you have no objection.' He looked at her sharply. 'But you haven't, of course.' Again the touch of arrogance.

She gave him a level glance. 'Dr Doelsma, I ken fine that there's many a good nurse here in this hospital, better than I, who would nurse your mother devotedly.'

He looked at her in amazement. 'Are you refusing, Maggy?'

'Aye, sir, I'm refusing.'

He said in a kind of wonder, 'Do you not like us?'

It was her turn to look amazed. 'Gracious goodness, Doctor, I like you fine—the both of you.'

'So it is personal reasons which make you refuse?'

She considered a minute. 'Yes, I suppose you might say that.'

He said sharply, 'Selfish reasons?'

Maggy sat quite still, looking at the frowning face, then got up slowly. 'Ye've no right to speak to me like that, sir. Now if ye'll excuse me, I'll away to my supper.'

Without a word he stood up, opened the door for her, and stood watching while she spoke to Nurse Sims and then went downstairs.

Her gay and animated manner at supper caused her friends to look askance. Maggy, for all her size, perhaps because of it, was known to be rather shy and retiring. Those who knew her well realised that she was in a dreadful temper. She did indeed go back to the ward with little sparks of rage in her eyes, and pink cheeks; most of the rage was against herself. She opened her office door and stood staring. The little room seemed full of people—Sir Charles Warren, Matron and Dr Doelsma. She looked at him down her beautiful nose and then turned her back, waiting for someone to speak.

Matron began: 'Er—Sister MacFergus, we won't keep you from your work, but I am sure that this little matter can be cleared up in a few moments. I am certain that your reasons for not going to Holland are given from the highest of motives, but I can assure you that you need have no qualms about leaving the ward. It is unusual, I admit, for a Ward Sister to take over a private case; but Sir Charles wishes it, and it can be arranged quite simply.' She inflated her bosom and nodded briskly, signifying that it was now Maggy's turn to speak.

They were all three looking at her, Matron with the certain air of a woman who had stated her case and expected no argument. Sir Charles with a shrewd twinkle, and Dr Doelsma with a smile. How dared he? Maggy gave him a baleful stare and turned a shoulder to him again.

'I should be glad if you would take on Mevrouw Doelsma, Maggy.' It was Sir Charles, at his most wheedling. 'She is a lifelong friend of mine; I want her to have the best attention there is, and I consider you are the one to give it. As a personal favour, Maggy.'

She liked and admired Sir Charles; she could not refuse him. He was also senior consultant of the hospital, and she a Ward Sister, there to do her work under his guidance and carry out his orders.

'If you wish it, Sir Charles, I'll be glad to go with Mevrouw Doelsma.'

He beamed at her. 'Splendid! I'm sure that Matron will see you later and fix up all the details. I think you should go in about ten days' time, don't you. Paul?'

Maggy didn't look round when Dr Doelsma answered, nor when he said,

'May I have a few words with Sister, Matron? I promise I won't keep her for more than a minute.'

He ushered her and Sir Charles out of the little room and stood in the open doorway, contemplating Maggy's very straight back.

'You needn't be afraid,' he said blandly. 'I've left the door open this time.'

This remark had the effect of making her turn round to face him. She said with great hauteur and a rising colour,

'I do not wish to be reminded of that regrettable incident.'

He was instantly contrite. 'I'm sorry, indeed I am; not because I kissed you, but because I've made you angry. Forgive me, and for taking such shameful advantage of you just now. It was unfair, I know. But I want you to nurse Mother. I should have warned you that I like my own way, and go to any lengths to get it.' He waited a moment, but she did not speak. 'My mother is normally a bright and happy woman, but now she had been badly frightened. She hides her fear, but only when you or I are with her does she lose it. She is a sensible woman; in time she will overcome it, and forget. Until then, she needs help. She likes you, Maggy, and trusts you—as I do. Thank you for consenting to come.'

Maggy was still looking out of the window, facing a fact which could no longer be ignored. She was hopelessly in love with Dr Doelsma; and while her good sense counselled her to take the prudent action to withdrawing her consent and never seeing him again, the delightful prospect of being with him, perhaps frequently, for the next few weeks was impossible to ignore. Before she could change her mind, she turned round and said quietly,

'I'll be glad to go with your mother, Dr Doelsma, and stay with her until she is well again.'

He had been looking rather stern; now his whole face lighted up.

'You can't know how pleased I am that you will be at Oudehof with my mother. Come and tell her yourself, won't you?'

She was glad of her decision when she saw Mevrouw Doelsma, who took her hand and said, 'I'll never be able to thank you, my dear. I thought perhaps you wouldn't want to come—it will a dull life for you after the rush and bustle here.'

Maggy assured her that that was just what she would like, and went away to give the report to the night nurse. Before she went off duty she told a bewildered junior nurse to take all the roses from the office and carry them to the geriatric ward, and waited until the little room was once more bare. In her room, she took the remaining flowers over to the front lodge to George, whose wife was ill. She wasn't to know that Dr Doelsma would see them on his way out, and such were her feelings that she wouldn't have cared.

She cried slow bitter tears for a long time before she went to sleep that night.

CHAPTER FOUR

MAGGY SENSED that there was something amiss as soon as she got to her office the next morning. The night nurse looked nervous, even Williams looked worried. Maggy sat down at her desk. 'I'll have the report first, Nurse, shall I? Then you can tell me what's gone wrong.' She gave her an encouraging smile and opened the book. The report duly given and commented upon, the bad news came tumbling out. Madame Riveau had gone. It had happened during the busy period between six and seven, when the nurses were fully occupied with teas, bedpans, washing patients, giving medicines, changing beds... Madame Riveau had got up and dressed, unseen, what with screens being pulled and patients who were well enough walking up and down the ward to the bathroom. The first the nurses had known of it was the commotion caused by the two Riveau men, who, it seemed, had come into the ward via the fire escape. They had walked off with Madame Riveau before anything could be done. By the time the nurse had rung through to the porter, they had already gone, using the Casualty entrance. The nurse there, busy herself, had thought they were relatives who had spent the night with one of the ill patients.

'I'll have to let the Office know, and Matron,' said

Maggy. 'Write a statement, Nurse, and I'll sign it too, and take it along to Matron. It was no fault of yours. She's been a difficult patient and her husband has been wanting her home for a long time now. She was due out tomorrow morning anyway.' She sighed with relief at the thought that she would not have to meet those awful men again.

The days slipped by. Matron had told her that she would probably be in Holland for four weeks, perhaps a little longer; a relief Sister would run the ward until her return. Maggy wrote to her parents in Scotland, got herself a passport and looked through her clothes, openly envied by every nurse in the hospital.

It was arranged that they should travel on a morning plane. An ambulance took Mevrouw Doelsma and Maggy, very neat in her uniform and little cape, to the airport, where they were met by Sir Charles who had elected to see them off. Maggy had been surprised to see Dr Doelsma waiting with him when they arrived, but beyond a brief good morning he said nothing, but went away to see to the luggage. She had not anticipated that he would be travelling with them, indeed she had not known that he was in England. There was, she admitted to herself, no reason why he should have informed her of his plans. She spent the next ten minutes or so installing her patient and herself on the KLM plane. In this she had the good offices of the stewardess and between them Mevrouw Doelsma was made comfortable, reassured and generally made much of. Maggy was surprised to find Sir

Charles at her elbow; in answer to her enquiring look, he said,

'No. I'm not coming with you—but Paul will be. I was allowed to make sure that everything was all right before take-off.' He stayed a few minutes, and then took his leave, saying,

'You'll do, Henrietta. I'll be over to see you as soon as I can spare time for a holiday. Have a good trip—you too, Maggy, and I hope you enjoy your stay in Friesland.' He waved cheerfully from the door.

Mevrouw Doelsma watched Maggy fixing the portable oxygen cylinder so that it could be got at quickly and easily if it was wanted. She caught her eye and smiled and said,

'What a nuisance I'm being to everyone.' The smile flickered and went out. Her voice faltered. 'I hope you don't have to use it, Maggy.'

'Och, no,' Maggy said comfortably. 'It's like taking an umbrella with you to keep off the rain.'

Her patient giggled, and Paul, who had just entered the plane, decided that Maggy was indeed a blessing, with her calm efficient ways and her soothing Highland voice. He stowed away his medical bag and took the seat by his mother, leaving the window seat for Maggy. Having adjusted their seat belts, he talked gently about nothing in particular until they were airborne, when he opened *The Times* and a Dutch magazine called *Elsevier,* and became immersed in reading them. However, from time to time his eye strayed to Maggy, guarding her patient like a hawk, but finding time to glance out of the porthole with wide eyes.

'Have you not flown before, Sister?' he asked casually.

She looked across at him, her eyes alight with excitement.

'No, never. I've never left England before.' As she said it she realised how amusing she must be to the much-travelled doctor. She looked at him again to see if he was laughing at her, but he wasn't.

'We must make certain that you see as much of Holland as possible before you go back home.'

He became immersed in his papers again, but presently, when his mother went to sleep, he folded them carefully and crossed over to the seat beside Maggy. The coast of Holland was visible; he leant across her, and started to point out landmarks. Their heads were very close together. Maggy kept her gaze on the view below her, not hearing a word of what he was saying, but thinking of the weeks ahead.

The plane touched down at Schiphol, and with a minimum of delay and a maximum of efficiency Madame Doelsma was transferred to a small smart ambulance with rakish lines. Maggy was too occupied with her patient to do more than give a hasty look round. There was no sign of the doctor; she supposed he was seeing about their luggage. The white-coated ambulance driver prepared to shut them in, and said something to Maggy, who looked blank. Madame Doelsma murmured something and he laughed and looked at Maggy and nodded and gave the thumbs-up sign, the friendly little gesture warmed her heart.

As soon as the door was shut, she began a systematic search of the ambulance, so that she would be familiar with the equipment if she should need it. When she had made a thorough inspection she sat herself down on the collapsible seat by her patient. It was a very small seat; she wriggled experimentally, reflecting on the long journey ahead of them, Mevrouw Doelsma was lying with her eyes closed, so Maggy allowed her attention to wander out of the window in the door of the ambulance. Drawn up within a few yards of their own vehicle was an ink-blue Rolls-Royce convertible. Dr Doelsma, hands in pockets, was leaning against its well-bred bonnet, talking to an elderly man by the boot, who was supervising the stowing away of the luggage. When this had been done to his entire satisfaction, the elderly man tipped the porter and went round to the doctor. Maggy watched with interest while they carried on another short conversation, at the end of which the elderly man sketched a vague salute and disappeared round the corner of the airport building, while the doctor strolled over to the ambulance and opened the door. He nodded briefly at Maggy, and addressed himself to his mother, who had opened her eyes at the sound of the door opening.

'Another hour or two, and we'll be home, dear. Pratt sends his regards; he and Mrs Pratt hope to see you soon.' He transferred his gaze to Maggy, who looked tranquilly back at him. 'It's roughly a hundred and forty miles.' he said. 'The ambulance will take about four hours to do the journey. I believe there is everything you require here; there's a flask of coffee...' He stopped as she nodded. 'Of course, you would have discovered that for yourself. I'll travel behind you. If you want anything, anything at all, wave through the back window.' He added dryly. 'Wave to me first, won't you, before you ask the driver to stop, otherwise I might run into you.'

Maggy nodded meekly, hiding a slight scorn. Presumably he thought that, outside nursing, she was a fool.

'What word do I use to stop the driver?' she asked sensibly.

He smiled. 'Stop. It's the same word; but in any case I've warned him to pull up if you appear worried.' He looked her up and down, and said with some amusement,

'The seat is too small for you, isn't it? I'm afraid they don't cater for Amazons. Shall I find you a cushion?'

His solicitude met with a cold reception. She drew her black brows together and said tartly,

'I thank you, no, sir. I'm well able to look after myself.'

His eyes widened with laughter. 'But of course, Sister, I apologise if I implied otherwise.'

She felt her cheeks redden as he turned away to speak to his mother before shutting the door and going back to his car.

The journey seemed endless. Mevrouw Doelsma possessed herself of one of Maggy's hands, sighed contentedly and went to sleep. Maggy looked out of the window, trying to see the names of the towns and villages which they went through—not always successfully. The Rolls kept at a discreet distance behind them, and she felt a pang of sympathy for the doctor compelled as he was to travel at such a moderate speed.

The country was charming—bright with autumn colours, flat as a plate and incredibly tidy. As they slowed down through the towns she was able to glimpse the small gabled houses, living proofs of a long-dead age, and seemingly too diminutive to house a normal family; whereas the churches were so vast that she could only assume that they stood forlorn and half empty each Sunday.

It had been explained to her that they would be taking the eastern road to Oudehof. Maggy had looked up the route carefully beforehand, but as much of it led along the main motorways, which skirted the towns, her carefully acquired knowledge was not of much use to her. However, after a little time they entered country reminiscent of the New Forest and she at last knew where she was. The *Veluwe*—the road was bordered by charming thatched houses, quite small, but modern and enclosed in large gardens so perfect that she guessed that they must be occupied by the wealthy. The road widened again, and they emerged into rolling meadowlands with tantalising glimpses of small towns. She looked at her watch—there was, she reckoned, less than an hour of the journey to go. Mevrouw Doelsma woke up and asked where they were, and shortly after Maggy caught sight of a fast disappearing signpost.

'Heerenveen,' said Maggy. 'That's not far from Oudehof, is it?'

'No, we're nearly home, Maggy. We turn off on the road to Balk; Oudehof is a mile or two this side of the village.' She smiled faintly. 'You know, dear, I thought, once or twice in the hospital, that I should never see Oudehof again. I do hope you are going to be happy there—it is very quiet, and you are so young and pretty, you should be having fun.'

Maggy laughed rather wistfully. 'Dinna worry, Mevrouw Doelsma, I'll not miss what I seldom had.'

Her patient raised her eyebrows. 'But, Maggy... I've not liked to ask you before, but surely you must have boy-friends, or one special one?'

Maggy chuckled. 'Nay, where will I find a wee man to top my size?' Her gaze fell on the sleek car loitering behind the ambulance and she looked away quickly with pink cheeks. 'I'll be very happy, Mevrouw Doelsma; I've never been in a foreign land, and everything is strange and exciting to me.'

She broke off as the ambulance turned off at right angles from the main road. Her patient became quite animated.

'Maggy, tell me anything you see, so that I know where we are.'

They travelled several kilometres thus, with Maggy describing windmills, canals, and houses as they passed them, until they turned off the narrow road through a pair of magnificent wrought iron gates and bowled along a semi-circular drive—Maggy could just see its other end sweeping back to the road again via another pair of gates. She twisted round and craned her neck to see through the tiny window behind the driver, and caught her first glimpse of Oudehof. It was red brick, square, and so symmetrical that it appeared to have been cut out of cardboard, and then stuck on to the surrounding countryside. There was an imposing door, approached by double steps, and flanked by large flat windows—the same windows crossed the face of the house in two neat rows above the door, capped by a steep roof. The house had the air of having been there a long time, and had every intention of remaining just as it was for a comfortable forever.

The ambulance drew up in front of the entrance, and before the driver was out of his seat, the Rolls had slid to a halt a couple of feet behind them, and it was the doctor who opened the door. His eyes went at once to his mother.

'All right, Mama? I'll carry you up to your room.' He slid the stretcher partly out on its runners, picked her up in his arms, and strode off to the door, where a small group of people had gathered.

Maggy, collecting the odds and ends of their journey, thought how much nicer it would have been if he had at least suggested that she should go with them. She eyed the figures in the doorway, feeling shy. Doubtless Dr Doelsma expected her to follow him. She walked across the broad sweep of the drive towards the door, and as she did so one of the people standing detached himself and came to meet her. He was grey-haired and pleasant-faced, and when he spoke she realised he was English. 'I'm Pratt, the butler, Sister.' He took her case and her cloak; he didn't smile, but she sensed his friendliness towards her. 'I'll take you to Madam's rooms, and later on, if you will ring, Mrs Pratt will take you to your room.'

She gave him a grateful glance and followed him into the hall. It was square and rather dim, and the black and white tiled floor gleamed richly underfoot. The walls were panelled and hung with portraits. There were doors leading off on either side, and a broad staircase, elaborately carved, rose from the back of the hall to a half-landing, and then branched off on either side to the floor above. Maggy found herself gently ushered past the handful of men and women gathered near the door and led upstairs to a broad corridor. He crossed this and knocked on a door decorated with swags of fruit and flowers, delicately carved in the wood. The doctor's voice answered and Pratt opened the door and ushered her in. Mevrouw Doelsma was lying on a fourposter bed; the doctor was in the act of covering her with a rug and looked over his shoulder at Maggy. He spoke rather testily. 'Why have you been so long?'

Maggy went over to the bed and eyed him coldly across it.

'Because, unlike you, sir, I didn't ken the way around the house.'

There was a faint giggle from the bed. 'You deserved that, Paul.'

A reluctant smile tugged at the corner of his mouth. 'I'm sorry, Sister MacFergus. I had no intention of giving you such a poor welcome to Oudehof. If you would be kind enough to settle my mother in bed, I'll find Mrs Pratt and tell her to bring up tea.'

He disappeared, and Maggy lost no time in getting Mevrouw Doelsma comfortable, thinking as she did so that it must be very pleasant to sleep between such fine linen sheets, monogrammed and embroidered; each of the square pillows was embellished with lace, and the counterpane of peach and silver brocade seemed to her eye to be old but still magnificent. Tea came just as she was finished, and, rather to her surprise, the doctor as well. He introduced Mrs Pratt after she had greeted her mistress with every sign of delight, and when she had puffed her good-natured person away, said,

'Will you pour out, Maggy?' He pulled up a chair to the small drum table where the tea tray had been set, and waved her to it. She hesitated. 'Will ye no' like to have tea together, sir? I have to unpack.'

'Certainly you must unpack, but only after we've had some tea. Do please pour out.'

She found herself yielding to his compelling charm, and took her place at the table, pouring tea from a magnificent silver tea-pot into paper-thin china cups. The small meal was a lighthearted affair, and Maggy relaxed despite herself after a few minutes of the doctor's easy conversation, forgetting to be shy of her rather grand surroundings, so that an hour slipped away before he suggested that she might like to see her room and unpack.

Mrs Pratt, summoned once more, led her through

a door leading from her patient's room into another similar one, equally beautifully furnished. From here they went into the corridor, where Mrs Pratt opened another door, revealing a luxurious bathroom.

'This will be for your own use while you are here, Sister, and please ask me or Pratt for anything you may require.' The housekeeper nodded and smiled, and puffed back into the bedroom; she was a stout little woman, but very light and active on her feet. Expressing the hope that Maggy would be very happy while she was at Oudehof, she went away, leaving her to unpack and put her clothes away in the vast drawers and closets, where they were immediately lost in a luxurious vastness. When Maggy had tidied herself she went back to Mevrouw Doelsma's room, where the doctor was lounging in a very large chair by the window; he got up and she went in, saying,

'Ah, Sister, there are one or two things to discuss, are there not?' There was no trace of the charming friendly man with whom she had had tea; rather he was the bland consultant, giving instructions to his nurse—which, she supposed, in all fairness, was their correct relationship. They walked over to the window and she listened composedly to his directions. 'My mother's own doctor will call tomorrow morning; if he suggests any changes you will of course follow his wishes. Now I expect you wish to get my mother ready for the night—I suggest that she has a really long sleep. Order anything you may require from Mrs Pratt.' He smiled briefly at her, went over to bed and kissed his mother and wished her goodnight, and left the room.

Mevrouw Doelsma was tired but happy. Maggy dallied over the preparations for bed and stayed with her while she ate her supper, then, leaving a bedside lamp burning and one or two books within reach, prepared to take the tray downstairs. Her patient, looking extremely comfortable against her pillows, said,

'Now go down and have dinner, Maggy. I shall be all right. I'll ring if I want you.'

Maggy went downstairs with the tray to be met with a rather shocked Pratt, who assured her that there was no need for her to be carrying trays and that she had only to ring when she needed anything done. He put the tray down on a marble-topped wall table in the hall, and opened a pair of double doors and showed her into the dining room, led her to the vast table and pulled out her chair.

'Master Paul has gone back to Leiden, Sister. He wished you good night and hopes that you will be comfortable.'

Maggy ate the delicious meal, barely noticing what was on her plate. The room was large and of a rich unobtrusive splendour; she felt lost and very lonely in it. Why had she imagined that the doctor would stay—at least to dine? She was, after all, only the nurse. She sat at the gleaming mahogany table, drinking her coffee and wishing she had never come. She must have been mad to have consented to the doctor's wishes, she should have had nothing more to do with him, and then forgotten him completely. Upon reflection, she admitted to herself that this would have been very difficult indeed. She got up and strolled over to the window; it was a lovely moonlit evening, she could see quite clearly across the gardens to the country beyond. She closed her eyes and thought of her own lonely beautiful Highlands; she longed to be there, walking the dogs, with her home in the valley below; a small safe refuge where she could shut out the rest of the world—she opened her eyes—only she wouldn't be able to shut out Paul.

Maggy got up the next morning after a night of dreams and bouts of heavy sleep, and went to the window. It was a lovely morning; the country around was calm and peaceful, she could see a great distance in every direction. She dressed and went to see how her patient did.

Mevrouw Doelsma, after a sound night's sleep, was in the best of spirits. The day passed happily enough, as did the next two days. Maggy found that she had a fair amount of time to herself while her patient rested. Mrs Pratt took her on a tour of the house, which, she learned, was more than two hundred years old. A great deal of the furniture was almost as old too, and very beautiful. Maggy spent a long time studying the portraits on the walls. Several of them were very obvious ancestors of the doctor. She was surprised to find that there was an extensive park behind the house, and a sizeable stable block, which she made up her mind she would explore one day. She had already made friends with the gardeners and Piet, the groom, who spoke no English, but made things surprisingly clear by means of nods and smiles.

Mevrouw Doelsma was proving herself to be an excellent patient and progressing well, but Maggy took care not to stray too far from the house. They spent a long time in each other's company, and Maggy listened enthralled to her patient recounting the history of the house and the family. Of the doctor there was no sign. His mother spoke of him frequently, but gave no clue as to his whereabouts.

Maggy went to bed at the end of her fourth day there resigned to the possibility of not seeing him again. She presumed that he would come to see his mother, but it would be unlikely that he would seek her out other than to give her his instructions, and enquire as to his mother's condition. She told herself not to cry for the moon, and resolved to enjoy herself as far as possible while she was in Holland.

CHAPTER FIVE

MAGGY SUPPOSED IT was the wind that wakened
her—it was sighing and rustling around the old house;
she supposed that she would get used to it in a day
or so. She lay listening to it, and gradually became
aware of another sound. She sat up in bed and looked
at her watch. Who would be walking about at half
past one in the morning? She strained her ears and
was sure that she heard voices. She got out of bed,
pulled on her dressing gown and slippers, and went
to the door and peered into the corridor. There was a
dim light at the head of the stairs, and nothing to be
seen, but the sounds, faint as a whisper, were still
playing a duet with the wind. Maggy left the door
open and padded across her room and into that of her
patient. Mevrouw Doelsma was sleeping quietly.
Maggy slid into the corridor and down the stairs; the
dining room door was slightly open and there was a
thin ribbon of light gleaming palely from it. She
crossed the hall, thoughtfully picking up a poker as
she passed the massive stove against one wall. The
dining room was in darkness, but the kitchen beyond
was brightly lit. She went steadily towards the partly
open door, swallowing fear with a throat gone dry,
and pushed it open. There were two people in the
kitchen; one of them was Dr Doelsma. He and a very

pretty girl were sitting side by side on the kitchen table in the middle of the room. He looked over his shoulder as Maggy went in, put down the mug he was holding, and got to his feet.

'Sister MacFergus, were we making so much noise?' He caught sight of the poker and came forward and took it from her. 'An Amazon, and armed!' he murmured with a twinkle, then turned to the girl still sitting on the table and said casually,

'Stien, this is Sister MacFergus, of whom I told you.' He smiled at Maggy, standing pokerless and awkward between the door and the kitchen table. 'May I introduce Juffrouw Stien van der Duren from Utrecht hospital?'

The girl got off the table and came over to Maggy, holding out her hand. She was small, barely up to Maggy's shoulder, and slim and very pretty with fair hair hanging in a shining curtain to her shoulders. Maggy shook hands, aware of her own junoesque proportions enveloped rather bunchily in a sensible dressing gown.

'How do you do,' she said rather stiffly. 'I'm sorry I disturbed you. I heard noises and thought I should see who it was. I'll wish you both a good night.'

She turned to the door, the dignified exit she had planned quite spoiled by a chair which she hadn't noticed and which she now tripped over. The doctor's large hand prevented her from falling, but she didn't look at him as she brushed past him with a muttered, 'My thanks to the doctor.'

As she went up the stairs she heard the girl's soft laughter.

Maggy awoke early and dressed, made her patient comfortable with her morning tea, and went down to get her own breakfast. Picking up her second cup of coffee, she took it to the window and stood looking out across the park. Presently she became aware of two people cantering towards the house, and had no difficulty in recognising them. The doctor, on a raw-boned bay worthy of his size, was slightly ahead, but drew in his mount so that his companion could catch up with him. Stien, Maggy noted sourly, looked as attractive on horseback as she did on her two feet. She watched them turn the corner of the house, talking animatedly, before going back to the table, banging her cup and saucer down on it, and going to the door. She had her hand on its big brass handle when she heard her name. Dr Doelsma had come in through the french window.

'Good morning—I saw you at the window. Have you breakfasted?' He scanned the table. 'I hadn't expected you up so early.'

She stood very straight, her voice as crisp and severe as her uniform.

'Your mother likes her breakfast about this time. It's easier if I have mine first. I'm used to early rising, Dr Doelsma.'

He surveyed her coolly. 'I hope you were not too badly frightened last night, Maggy?'

The unfairness of this remark brought a vexed flush to her cheeks, but she answered in a level voice 'If I had been badly frightened, sir, I should not have left my bedroom.'

He raised his eyebrows and grinned at her and seemed about to say something further, but turned instead to the window where Stien had appeared. Maggy wished her a quick good morning and made her escape. As she went up the stairs she wondered, as she had wondered many times in the night, just who Stien was.

Mevrouw Doelsma didn't need much done for her, but she loved company. She talked happily about Paul, and spoke of Stien as though she had known her intimately for a long time. Maggy wanted very much to ask if they were engaged, but could not quite bring herself to do so.

The morning passed with only a brief visit from the doctor, who, as he entered the room, suggested that she might like to take advantage of his visit to have her coffee or go for a turn in the gardens, so that when she returned shortly, their conversation was limited to questions and answers of a purely professional nature.

Maggy had a solitary lunch, waited upon by Pratt, and then returned upstairs to settle her patient for her afternoon nap. That lady, thoroughly rested from her journey, and delighted at the prospect of getting up and going downstairs on the following day, was disposed to talk, and it was almost two o'clock before Maggy left her, changed into a kilt and sweater and went downstairs. As she passed through the hall, she heard voices and laughter from the dining room, and

supposed Dr Doelsma and Stien were having a late
lunch. Perhaps they hadn't cared to lunch with the
nurse. Maggy wondered if she should have asked to
have her meals in her room. She had done no private
nursing, and that aspect of it had not struck her. She
should have found out more about it before leaving
the hospital. However, it was too late now, so she
smiled at Pratt who had appeared to open the door
for her, and walked briskly down the drive towards
the road. The doctor was home; she felt that she could
safely go further afield for an hour or so.

The village was small—a cluster of houses, a few
small shops and a large church, which she found to
be locked. She bought some stamps, posted letters,
and purchased some local views. There were some of
Oudehof, so Maggy sent one to the nurses on her
ward, and one to Mrs Salt. The people she met were
pleasant and friendly, and though they spoke no English, were very helpful when it came to paying for
her purchases. She walked back feeling much happier
and less lonely.

She changed back into uniform and went to see
how Mevrouw Doelsma was feeling; she found her
awake and reading letters, which she put down as
Maggy went in.

'Did you have a good walk? Paul and Stien have
just gone—some play or other Stien wanted to see in
Amsterdam. They asked me to say goodbye to you.
Paul says that I may go for a check-up next week. He
suggests that we stay for a day or two in Leiden—he
has a house there—so that you can have a look round.

You'll want to see Amsterdam, and Leiden and Delft, and perhaps the Hague.'

She chattered on, while Maggy helped her to the chair by the small open fire.

'Shall we have tea, and discuss what we can do tomorrow? Paul thought that if it is fine, I might go out for an hour in the car. Do you drive, Maggy?'

Maggy nodded, 'Aye, I do.'

Her patient's eyes sparkled. 'Would you be all right here, do you think?'

Maggy considered. 'Aye, I think so.' She had driven her father's old Landrover over some shocking bad roads in Scotland in snow and ice and fog. It should be easy in Holland, with never a hill to see. The signs might present a problem, but she thought that they were international to a large extent, and driving on the other side of the road, although strange, should present no difficulties.

'I'd like fine to drive,' she said.

'And so you shall, my dear, but perhaps we had better let Pratt drive tomorrow, and then you can take the wheel for a time. He's rather fussy, I'm afraid—he prefers horses.'

Maggy poured second cups. 'That was a fine beast the doctor was riding this morning.'

'Cobber? Yes, though he takes a bit of riding, Paul tells me. Do you ride, Maggy?'

'Since I was a wee girl; but there's not much chance in London, so when I'm home, I often spend the day riding in the hills.'

'But, Maggy, you must ride here—there are three

or four horses in the stables. Ride every morning before breakfast. Pratt shall tell the groom.'

So it was settled, and early next morning Maggy
spent a magic hour exploring the country. Her mount
was not quite to her liking, however. Biddy was a
well-mannered roan with a middle-aged disposition,
and a dislike of any exercise harder than a canter.
There was a wide sweep of parkland behind the
house. Maggy longed to gallop over it, and Cobber,
she felt sure, would share her views.

The drive to Sneek after lunch was a great success.
The lakes sparkled in the autumn sunshine; they drove
slowly through the little town, and then turned into
the direction of Heerenveen. Pratt turned the car just
below the town into Oranjewoud, where the roads
were quiet, and changed places with Maggy. The car
was a Daimler Sovereign, and she drove it through
the wooded lanes before turning and going back the
way they had come. Pratt sat silently beside her, but
when she drew up before the door at Oudehof, gave
his opinion that her driving was as good as his own,
and he for his part felt quite happy about her taking
the car whenever she wanted it. This was indeed high
praise and she thanked him gratefully. While he was
having his tea later, he informed his wife that Sister
MacFergus was a well set up, sensible young lady,
and pretty too, if you liked your women big.

The next few days passed happily enough. Maggy
rode every morning and drove her patient, with Pratt
in attendance, round the countryside each afternoon.
There was no sign of Dr Doelsma; if his mother had

heard from him, she said nothing. Friends began to call, and Maggy, with time on her hands, spent some time in the stables, making friends with Cobber. He rolled a wicked eye at her, but took her sugar lumps and listened while she talked to him. She had every intention of riding him when she had the opportunity. It came sooner than she had expected, a couple of mornings later when she slipped out of the side door. There was a grey sky with a hint of rain and more than a hint of wind, and no one about in the stables. Without hesitation she went to Cobber's stall, saddled him and led him out into the back drive.

Half an hour later, horse and rider turned for home, girl and beast both happy and satisfied. Some way from the house, Maggy turned off the track they had been following, and once on the grass gave Cobber his head. He needed no urging, but broke into a gallop across the parkland. With easy skill Maggy pulled him back into a canter as they neared the house, and turned the corner of the house at a gentle walk.

Dr Doelsma was standing on the side door steps. He was dressed for riding and white with well-controlled rage. Maggy stopped Cobber in front of him, leaned forward and patted the horse's neck, and said in a small voice. 'Good morning, Dr Doelsma.' She had gone rather white too, but met his furious gaze bravely. He stood at his ease, looking her up and down. It had been raining for some time, and her hair hung in a damp pony-tail, and small mist-spangled curls framed her face. She was only too aware of the bedraggled appearance of her sweater and slacks, and her lack of make-up. She sat quite still, waiting for him to speak.

'How dare you take my horse?' His voice was very soft. 'No one rides Cobber but myself.'

'Aye, I know, Doctor. But he was in need of a good gallop, and I've done him no harm.' She lapsed into broad Scots: 'Dinna' fash yersel', sir, I ken well hoo to ride, and have done since I was a wee bairn.'

'So I am able to see for myself, but that is no excuse, I think.' His eyes were grey steel. 'I should like to shake you!' he added furiously. Maggy dismounted, and threw the bridle over one arm, and prepared to lead Cobber back to the stables.

'I'm sorry ye're disappointed at not getting your ride, Doctor, but it's as well. I'm thinking, for ye're in an awful rage. A good walk, now, is fine for the bad temper. I was not to know that ye'd be wanting Cobber, and please don't blame Pratt. I was earlier than usual this morning, and he knew nothing of this.'

She didn't wait for an answer, but led Cobber away without a backward glance.

She didn't see him again until after lunch—she had been taking her meals with Mevrouw Doelsma, but suggested that today it would be a good idea if she had hers in her room. Her patient agreed that she had a great deal to talk about with her son, mostly business, which could perhaps be better discussed if they were alone.

Accordingly, mother and son sat down to luncheon without Maggy. It wasn't until Paul looked up from his soup and enquired carelessly as to Maggy's whereabouts that Mevrouw Doelsma asked the question she had been pondering for most of the morning.

'What have you said to Maggy, Paul?'

He looked faintly annoyed. 'Nothing of consequence, Mama.'

'She's displeased you?'

'If you mean am I displeased with the nursing treatment she gives you, Mother—on the contrary, she is a splendid nurse. I am all admiration for her skill.'

His mother caught his eye. 'Please don't blame her, Paul. It was I who suggested she should drive in the first place, and Pratt says she handles the car to the manner born.'

Paul choked on his soup. 'The Daimler?' he enquired.

She nodded, then frowned. 'Wasn't that it?' She sounded worried. 'Is there something else?'

He said in an interested voice, 'I wasn't aware that Sister MacFergus had been driving the car. We can discuss that later. She was out riding this morning...' His mother interrupted eagerly.

'Yes, dear. She goes out every morning; she rides well, I believe. Did you join her?'

Her son smiled reluctantly. 'I had no opportunity, Mama, to do so. Maggy was riding Cobber.'

Mevrouw Doelsma gasped, 'Good heavens, Paul! Cobber's far too strong for her. Was she all right?'

The doctor inspected the roast partridge on his plate before replying.

'You are alarmed for Sister MacFergus, my dear mother, whereas I was alarmed for Cobber.'

His mother looked indignant.

'Paul, sometimes I have no patience with you! I hope that one day, when you do fall in love, it will be with a woman who refuses to be ignored for a horse!'

This remark made her son laugh and restored his good humour, so that the rest of the meal was spent cheerfully enough making plans for her forthcoming trip to Leiden.

After their coffee, Mevrouw Doelsma declared her intention of going to the kitchen and having a word with Mrs Pratt. Paul lighted his pipe and strolled across to his study. Maggy was coming down the stairs with her tray as he crossed the hall. She reddened when she saw him, but said nothing when he took the tray from her and said quite gently,

'You have no need to carry trays, Maggy.' He put it down, and went on, 'Will you come into the study for a moment?'

He opened the door for her, and she went in, still saying nothing. She had not been in the room before. It was lofty, with large windows overlooking the garden at the side of the house. The walls were panelled, and besides the enormous desk it was furnished with a selection of comfortable leather armchairs, piled untidily with books and papers which the shelves around the walls could no longer accommodate.

'Sit down, Sister,' he said quietly.

Maggy sat, her large capable hands folded in her white starched lap, her serene manner hiding her chaotic thoughts.

He came and stood in front of her, his hands in his pockets, and she studied his shoes—nice hand-made ones, not too new. She had no doubt that he was looking at her, and very crossly too, she was certain. She had no intention of meeting his gaze.

When he spoke, his voice was still quiet, but it sounded friendly.

'Maggy, I must beg your pardon.'

Her intention not to look at him was forgotten in her astonishment. Her head jerked back so that her eyes could verify what her ears had heard. Her mouth hung very slightly open.

'I had no right to speak to you as I did this morning; it was most uncivil of me—' he paused. She smiled warmly at him, but he chose to ignore this, looking severely over her head. 'Nevertheless, I must ask you not to ride Cobber unless I give my permission.'

Maggy stiffened slightly. 'I should not have ridden him; I have said I was sorry, sir...but I can manage him.' She encountered his furious glance, and stopped.

'Are you suggesting that you should ride Cobber whenever you wish? Indeed, Sister MacFergus, I hope that I am not an unreasonable man, but you must at least allow me my own horse!' He sounded as angry as he looked. 'My mother tells me that you have been driving the Daimler. You have your driving licence with you. I hope? I must take Pratt's word for it that you are competent, I suppose.' He spoke with an icy

politeness; he had quite forgotten that only a few
minutes before he had been begging her pardon.

Maggy rose to her feet, brows a rigid line above
blazing eyes. It was obvious that she had inherited the
temper of the more belligerent of her Highland forebears.

'Ye're an angry wee man, Doctor, and not worth
the answering, and I'm none so mild mesel' at the
present.'

He watched while she crossed to the door and went
out, closing it very quietly behind her, and presently
began to laugh.

Maggy tucked her patient up for her afternoon nap,
and went to her room to write letters; she thought that
the less she saw of the doctor, for a time at least, the
better. She was feeling ashamed of herself. She had
behaved badly, and now she would have to apologise;
he might even ask her to return to England. She
stopped writing, aghast at the idea, until common
sense told her that he was unlikely to take such a step.
He had only to tell Pratt and the groom that he didn't
wish her to drive the car or ride. Maggy fancied that
he was a man who expected and got his wishes
obeyed. She would have to walk. She looked out of
the window at the pleasant, placid scenery, stretching
away flatly to the horizon, and suddenly wanted hills
and heather; she struggled with a strong desire to
burst into tears, and presently sat down and wrote
several long and slightly mendacious letters.

She had tea with Mevrouw Doelsma and then

helped her downstairs to the front door, where Pratt was waiting to take them for a drive. Maggy settled her patient in the back seat and got in beside her, saying: 'I'd like to sit beside you today, I can't enjoy the scenery if I'm driving.'

Mevrouw Doelsma agreed that this was a good idea, and the first part of the journey was passed pleasantly discussing the various landmarks they passed. Presently Maggy brought the conversation round to the proposed trip to Leiden, which interesting topic kept them engrossed until their return to Oudehof.

When they went down to dinner, the doctor was waiting for them in the drawing room. He greeted them pleasantly, and enquired after his mother's day. During dinner he included Maggy meticulously in the conversation, treating her with a frosty politeness which chilled her to the bone. When she had settled Mevrouw Doelsma by the fire once more, she excused herself on the pretext of writing letters, and escaped to her room. When she returned an hour later, she found them playing bézique and laughing a great deal; it was impossible not to notice how different the doctor looked when he laughed. Maggy thought wistfully that it would be fun to laugh with him; the possibility seemed unlikely.

Mevrouw Doelsma took a long time to put to bed— pills and blood pressure, TPR and checking carefully that her ankles hadn't swollen. At last she was lying comfortably against her pillows, with the bedside lamp adjusted, and book, glasses and bell all within reach. They wished each other a friendly goodnight, and Maggy went to her own room and to bed. She didn't think Dr Doelsma was expecting her downstairs again.

The bell woke her at once; she was out of bed, scuffing her feet into her slippers and putting on her dressing gown as she went. Mevrouw Doelsma looked small and white in the big bed, and there were beads of sweat on her forehead; her eyes implored Maggy, who took one all-embracing, understanding look and fetched a basin. She lifted Mevrouw Doelsma with one strong young arm and held her comfortably in its circle.

'That delicious lobster ye had for dinner,' she said practically. 'Ye'll feel better in a wee moment, and when ye are, I'll fetch the doctor...'

'I'm here.' His voice came from behind her.

She didn't turn round, but said in a sensible voice,

'If you'll go to the other side of the bed and hold Mevrouw Doelsma while I change the bowl...?'

He complied, and she heard him talking low-voiced to his mother. When she returned to the bedside, he had his mother's wrist in his fingers. Maggy fetched the BP box and wound the cuff on to Mevrouw Doelsma's arm, saying comfortably,

'You don't need to worry; the doctor'll tell you it's bilious ye've been.'

She handed the stethoscope across the bed to him, and tossed her hair, hanging loose around her shoulders and down her back; she was completely unselfconscious, intent only on her patient.

Dr Doelsma examined his mother, then handed the stethoscope back to Maggy without looking at her.

'Maggy's right, Mama. You've no need to worry; it's not a heart attack, it's lobster! You feel better already, don't you?'

His mother nodded. 'How silly of me! I'm so sorry to have got you both out of bed for nothing.'

'I'm not minding,' said Maggy calmly, 'and I doubt the doctor's minding either.' She looked across the bed. 'Will you be kind enough to support your mother, sir, while I shake up the pillows?' She pushed up her dressing gown sleeves the better to work. The cord of her dressing gown had worked loose too, she undid it and wrapped the garment closely around her, pulling the cord tightly around her neat waist. The simple action, guilelessly done, made her seem very young and childlike despite her size. She shook the pillows with a vigorous grace, and having rearranged them to her satisfaction waited while the doctor laid his mother back amongst them.

'There,' she said cheerfully, 'I'll sponge your face and hands, and make you a cup of tea, and you'll be asleep again in ten minutes or so.'

She padded noiselessly around the big room collecting what she needed, and went back to the bed to find the doctor sitting on its edge, his mother's hand in his large one. He looked quite different; his rather tousled hair made him look very young, despite the elegant silk dressing gown he was wearing. They smiled at each other in a comfortable friendly fashion and he got up.

'I'll go and put the kettle on. I'll be back in ten minutes, will that be all right?'

Half an hour later Mevrouw Doelsma, now pleasantly sleepy, said goodnight for the second time. Her son had brought a cup of tea, and told her bracingly that there was nothing for her to worry about, and she could now go to sleep. He kissed her cheek gently, said goodnight and went away, leaving Maggy to switch on the small night lamp before she too went to her room.

It had become quite chilly. She looked at her watch, it was almost three o'clock. She got the cooling bottle from her bed and crept downstairs to fill it. There was a lamp burning in the hall, but the dining room was in darkness. Maggy made her away through it to the kitchen door and opened it. It looked very cosy. There was a brown earthenware tea-pot on the table, with cups and saucers, and a milk jug and sugar bowl. Dr Doelsma was making toast. He looked up.

'Ah, there you are! I was going to bring it up to your room.' He saw the hot water bottle she was clutching, took the toast from toaster and said, 'Butter these, will you, while I fill your water bottle.' He didn't seem to expect an answer, so she obediently took the toast and buttered it, while he filled the hot water bottle and took it up to her room.

'I could have taken it,' Maggy said rather weakly when he came back.

'I'm sure you could.' He poured the tea. 'You are, I think, able to do most things very well.'

He handed her a cup, then fetched one of the old-fashioned ladderback chairs and set it behind her. 'Sit down.' He pulled up a second chair opposite to her, and handed her a slice of toast. They drank and munched in restful silence until he asked suddenly,

'Maggy do you like me?'

She put down her cup carefully. Her cheeks were pink, but she looked at him honestly.

'Aye, Doctor.'

'Even when I'm a wee evil-tempered man?'

The pinkness spread, but she replied steadily, 'Yes, even then.'

He went on conversationally, 'I like you—and admire your capabilities. Do you think we could be friends?' He held out a firm, well kept hand. 'I apologise again, Maggy.'

Maggy took the hand, and her own was immediately engulfed in its clasp; it felt very comforting. She said rather timidly, 'I was very rude; I'm sorry too. I thought you would send me back to England.'

He raised dark eyebrows at this, and then burst out laughing.

'My dear girl, surely you know that we would be lost without you? It's only because you are here that I am able to spend so much time in Leiden, and go to Utrecht whenever I wish.'

Stien lived in Utrecht. Of course, he would want to go there whenever he could. The thought hurt Maggy like a physical blow. She took a drink of hot strong tea and nearly choked at his next words.

'Will you ride with me tomorrow, Maggy?'

She didn't trust herself to look up, but said shyly, 'Thank you, I'd like to.'

'Er—I'll ride Cobber this time.' She did look up then, to find him smiling at her. He went on: 'But I'll tell Piet that you are to exercise him when I'm not here.' He took no notice of her attempt to thank him, but continued, 'I'm heaping coals of fire, aren't I? We'll take Mother for a run in the car tomorrow, and you shall drive; and don't think that I said that because I don't trust you to handle a car.'

He smiled again, and this time Maggy smiled back. She might not have his love, but to have his friendship would be worth a great deal to her. She wondered if Stien knew how lucky she was. She got up, collected the cups and saucers and stacked them neatly in the sink.

'I think I'll go to bed. Thank you for the tea, Dr Doelsma.' She stood, drooping with sleep, her hair hanging unheeded around her shoulders, her eyes enormous in a face devoid of make-up.

He looked at her briefly, then away again. 'Shall we say seven-thirty tomorrow?'

'Yes—that's provided Mevrouw Doelsma is all right.'

He opened the door for her, and Maggy said goodnight and walked sleepily across the dining room and out into the hall, and up the stairs. Long before Paul turned out the lights and went to his own room, she was fast asleep.

They rode for almost an hour before breakfast, the

doctor immaculate in riding kit, Maggy in her old slacks and thick sweater. She wasted a few moments wishing that she had other clothes to wear, then forgot about them as she swung herself easily on to Biddy's friendly back. If she envied the doctor Cobber, she gave no sign. As they turned for home, they broke into a brief gallop, and he held Cobber in, so that they raced neck and neck, until he allowed her to win by a short head. They pulled up outside the stables, and Maggy slid out of the saddle to make much of Biddy and give her the sugar lumps she loved. Her hair, which she had tied back in a ponytail, had come loose from its ribbon and her face glowed with happiness. She had been chattering to the doctor like an old friend. They left the horses with Piet, the groom, and went back to the house. At the door she paused.

'That was lovely,' she said. 'Thank you.'

He stood aside to let her pass, looking down at her. 'A delightful ride,' he said. 'We must do it again.'

They parted at the foot of the stairs, she to go to her room and change, and he to his breakfast. Maggy saw little of him that morning and he wasn't at lunch, but later that afternoon, when she and Mevrouw Doelsma went downstairs for their promised drive, they found him waiting for them beside the Rolls. He opened the door and helped his mother in, saying, 'Sit in front, Maggy, we'll change seats presently.'

She slid into the seat beside his. 'You don't mean that I'm to drive this car?' She was astounded. 'But it's a Rolls-Royce!'

'Don't you want to drive it?'

'Yes, very much; but I might be a shocking bad driver.'

'In which case I shall tell you so, and drive myself.'

He took the same route that Pratt had taken on their first drive, and once they had entered the comparative quiet of the Oranjewoud, he stopped, got out, and waited while Maggy took his place. Having made sure that she indeed knew what she was about, he suggested that she should keep on the road they were already upon, and that he would take over again when it joined the main Assen-Meppel road. Having given this piece of sound advice he half turned in his seat and engaged his mother in conversation. Maggy was thankful for his tack; she knew quite a lot about cars but found the Rolls a little awe-inspiring. She need not have worried, though, for the Rolls was a lady, and behaved like one. She relaxed. The doctor saw it and asked,

'Have you driven a Rolls before?'

'No. It's like wearing a model dress when you're used to Marks and Spencers—though I've not worn a model dress,' she added, incurably truthful.

'How long have you been driving?'

'Five—no, six years.'

'In the Highlands, I expect?'

'Yes, mostly. The roads are surprisingly good, excepting in the winter.' She eased the car past a farm wagon, and put her foot down gently; the road was straight and nothing in sight. He watched the needle creep round the speedometer and said,

'I gather that you have your advanced driver's certificate.' It was more of a statement than a question. She said. 'Yes, Doctor,' in a meek voice and he chuckled. 'No wonder you were annoyed with me!'

Maggy made no answer to this, but smiled, then slowed down to pass through a very small village straddling a canal, and obedient to his direction, turned into a right-handed fork towards the main road. Presently, when it was within sight, she drew in to the side of the road, stopped the car and looked at him enquiringly.

'Very nice, Maggy; you drive as well as I do.' He said it without conceit. He turned to his mother. 'If I didn't know better, I'd say that Maggy was wasted as a nurse, wouldn't you, Mama?'

Mevrouw Doelsma wouldn't agree to this. 'Maggy's a born nurse, but it would be nice for her,' she went on pensively, 'if she married a man with a Rolls-Royce.'

Maggy turned her head and looked intently at a view which hardly merited her prolonged scrutiny, and Dr Doelsma eyed her back with a slight smile and decided twinkle in his eyes. He said briskly, 'That shouldn't be too difficult.'

He got out of the car, and Maggy slid back to her own seat as he got in. 'Shall I get in beside Mevrouw Doelsma?' she asked, giving him a very fleeting look. But her patient declared that she was perfectly happy as she was, and Maggy was to stay where she was. She settled her length into the comfortable seat. 'Thank you, Doctor. It was wonderful.' He answered her with some trivial remark about the car, and by the time the car was on the main road they had entered into a lively discussion concerning various aspects of motoring, so that she forgot to be shy.

Once on the high road, clear of traffic, the doctor gathered speed. There was no limit on the motorway; the needle hovered on a hundred and sixty kilometers, and he asked. 'Nervous?'

'Not in the least,' Maggy retorted, 'but what about Mevrouw Doelsma?'

The little lady in the back seat laughed. 'I enjoy it. Pratt disapproves of me when I tell him to travel faster, but Paul knows how I like it.'

They flashed past a signpost and Dr Doelsma slowed down and turned into a narrow road.

'We'll go back to Heerenveen across country,' he said. 'The country's nothing like your Highlands, Maggy, but it's very pleasant.'

'That burst of speed was most enjoyable, Doctor.' Maggy sounded sedate. 'You'll be holding the same certificate as myself, I think.'

'*Hemel!*' He was half laughing. 'I've been guilty of showing off.'

'I was showing off too,' said Maggy, 'but it's plain that you're a better driver than I am.'

They all returned to Oudehof in excellent spirits, and later at dinner the doctor made himself so pleasant that as Maggy went upstairs, leaving him and his mother together, she reflected that she hadn't enjoyed herself so much for a long time.

Mother and son settled down to their usual game

of cards, and after a few minutes Mevrouw Doelsma remarked, 'Maggy drives very well, Paul.'

Paul took a trick. 'Yes, Mother. I noticed that you were sufficiently impressed to suggest that she should find a husband with a Rolls-Royce.'

His mother looked at her cards, wondering if she dared cheat. 'Yes, dear, such a good idea.' She cheated, and took the next trick, and he tried not to laugh.

'Mama, I have a Rolls-Royce.'

She looked up smilingly. 'Yes, dear, that's what I meant,' she said.

Paul stared at her. 'Mother dear, it has taken a whole evening of bright conversation to convince Maggy that that was not what you meant.'

His mother cheated again. 'The poor child! I only wanted to put an idea into your head, Paul.'

Paul took a trick and said, 'My dear, you surely know by now that the only ideas I act upon my own?' He smiled at her. 'If you cheat cleverly enough, you'll win this game!'

Maggy came back presently, and sat in a nice old Friesian chair, painted all over with small flowers. Her uniform looked very severe against it, but she suited the chair very well; it had been made for big men and women.

The doctor stacked the cards neatly.

'I must leave at six tomorrow morning, so we had better settle the arrangements for next week. I'll get an appointment for you, Mother, and Pratt can drive you both down. Stay for three or four days, and

Maggy can have a couple of days off and go sight-seeing. I'll be too busy to bring you back, but Pratt can fetch you whenever you want.'

His mother nodded. 'It will be nice to come to Leiden for a few days, even if it is to go to the hospital. And nice for Maggy too.'

He opened the door for them. 'It will be pleasant having you, Mother, and you too, Maggy. You'll exercise Cobber, won't you? I've spoken to Piet.' He kissed his mother, then took Maggy's hand and smiled down at her. 'I shall enjoy showing you my house in Leiden, Maggy.'

She felt suddenly shy, and murmured something incoherent. She wouldn't see him for a week, but then she would see him every day while she was in Leiden. She resolved, then and there, not to think about it.

They arrived in Leiden just in time for tea. The doctor wasn't home, but a housekeeper ushered them into the sitting room and went off to fetch their tea.

Maggy took a long look at the sitting room, and said, 'Please may I walk round?' Her patient laughed and said of course; so Maggy made Mevrouw Doelsma comfortable by the window, and started on an eager inspection of the room. It was large, stretching from front to back of the house, with folding doors dividing its length half way. The walls were panelled and the plaster ceiling festooned with swags of fruit and flowers. She could see that it had been furnished with care and an eye for detail. She wondered who had done this, and said so, out loud.

Mevrouw Doelsma smiled at her. 'I think you are feeling as I did the first time I saw this room. It's like walking into a Dutch interior, isn't it? All the furniture is antique and more or less as it was when the house was first built, and each generation has taken care to keep it that way. Paul loves every inch of it. He'll take you round, I expect, and tell you the history of everything, down to the last spoon.' She broke off as the housekeeper came in with the tea tray.

When she had gone, Maggy handed Mevrouw Doelsma her tea and sat herself down on the velvet covered window seat and drank her own out of a cup of very old Delft china of a delicate pinkish-mauve colour. She guessed that it was priceless, as was the silver tea tray, plain and solid, though the sugar bowl and cream jug were in the baroque style, very like those used at Oudehof. She struggled to remember who had made them, and was pleased when she recollected that it was Lely. They ate paper-thin sandwiches and little biscuits, richly covered in almonds, and there was a rich plum cake which reminded her of her mother's cooking.

They had almost finished when she saw the Rolls draw up outside, and the doctor mount the small flight of steps to his front door. He shut it firmly, as though he had come into his own little world, snug and secure. The thought crossed her mind that there should be small children running to meet him, and a wife waiting. She wished with all her heart that she could be that wife, and turned a face full of dreams to the door as he entered the room, so that he stood, staring.

By the time he had greeted his mother, however, and walked over to the window, Maggy was her usual self, calmly friendly, neat as a new pin in her uniform, ready to pour the fresh tea the housekeeper brought in, and answer readily the questions Paul put to her about their journey.

He turned to his mother. 'I'm sorry I couldn't be here when you arrived, Mama.'

'Yes, dear, so was I. I should have liked you to have seen Maggy when we came into this room.' She paused. 'It sounds absurd; it had the same effect on her as it did on me, Paul. She—gathered it to her. That sounds silly, but you know what I mean, I think?'

'Indeed I do.' He sat down in a beautiful carved chair with blue damask cushions, looking exactly like his ancestors on the wall behind him. But beyond this brief remark, he said no more about it, but entertained his mother with the kind of gossip she liked to hear, at the same time eating his way steadily through the plum cake. After a while he put his plate down.

'Have you been up to your rooms yet?'

Mevrouw Doelsma shook her head. 'No, dear. I thought I'd wait a while.'

'Then I'll show Maggy the house, and by the time we're done, I daresay you'll feel like going up.'

Maggy sat quietly in the window, taking little part in their conversation, but now she looked up as the doctor came towards her.

He held out a hand wordlessly, and she stood up and took it, and he led her through the door into the

hall. It was dim and cool, but not dreary. The black
and white tiles glowed underfoot with the patina of
age, as did the panelling, which stretched to the
heavily ornamental ceiling. A carved staircase rose
from the back of the hall, which narrowed to a passage leading to the back of the house, through a
graceful archway.

They crossed the hall, and entered a much smaller
room, with a similar panelling and ceiling, furnished
with a heavy oaken table and chairs. There was a
massive buffet against one wall, and in one corner, a
large circular stove, with a tile surround, rising to the
ceiling. Maggy lingered over the display of silver on
the buffet, fingering the flat serving dishes and tureens
with a loving hand, and only leaving them when the
doctor invited her to inspect the engraved goblets in
a corner cupboard. She held one, and marvelled at the
beauty of its cupids and roses. The doctor put it back
with its fellows and said,

'It was made by David Wolff for my great-great-
grandfather. He loved beautiful things. He was a doctor too.'

'Have there always been doctors in your family?'
Maggy wanted to know.

'For the last two hundred years or so, yes,' he answered. 'Before that we had land and ships and a
great many sheep. We still have the land, but no ships
and only the sheep we own on the farms.'

Maggy found this remark rather daunting; he
seemed even more removed from her world than be-

fore. She said hesitantly, 'I thought Friesland was famous for its cows.'

'So it is; I must take you to Leeuwarden one day and show you the statue of Mother Cow in the Zuiderplein. We have two farms in the Achterhoek—quite small ones run by cousins of mine. They find sheep pay better.'

He had opened a door as he was speaking and they entered the library. It was at the back of the house, and had ground-length windows opening out on to a small balcony overlooking a very small, beautifully kept garden which ran down to the edge of a small canal. Maggy walked round the shelves, looking at the books, and said over her shoulder, 'Would you not like to shut yourself in here for years and read all these books?'

He laughed. 'Well, I've read a great number of them. I daresay when I am a very old man, I shall take your advice and read the remainder.' He stood by the window, watching her browsing. 'Please feel free to come here whenever you wish, Maggy, and borrow anything you want.'

Maggy thanked him and followed him back into the hall, from whence they mounted the staircase which opened on to a square landing, lighted by the high window over the front door. He led the way down a small passage leading to the back of the house and opened a door.

'This will be your room. I hope you will be comfortable; anything you want my housekeeper, Anny, will gladly get for you.'

It overlooked the canal and the garden and was furnished charmingly in mahogany and chintz. There was a small fourposter bed against one wall. It had a curved canopy and a coverlet of silk and lace. Maggy had thought Oudehof a very grand place, but this house on the edge of the Rapenburg canal, although much smaller, was even more richly furnished.

The doctor showed her several more rooms, all equally beautiful. On the opposite side of the landing he passed a door, commenting that it was his room, and led her past an elaborately carved double door, remarking briefly that it was naturally not in use, as it was the master bedroom, thence to a small narrow staircase, carved with as much skill as the one they had already ascended. At the top of the stairs was a very small sitting room with painted walls, a replica of one of the rooms at Oudehof which an ancestor had had copied, so that he should be reminded of Friesland while he lived in Leiden. The remaining rooms were intercommunicating, with wooden bars fixed across the narrow windows. In the first room there was a rocking horse pushed into a corner. The furniture was simple, rather old-fashioned and very cosy. They stood close together in the doorway, looking at it.

'The nurseries,' said the doctor. 'There's room for six children and two nursemaids up here. There were only three of us, so we had plenty of room.'

Maggy nodded. She was looking at a magnificent doll's house and a row of dolls on a shelf. She said regretfully, 'They look so lonely.'

He smiled. 'I don't come up here very often, I'm afraid; but when I marry and have children, I expect I shall be up here a great deal.'

Maggy swallowed. 'Yes, of course,' she said in a colourless voice.

'There's another floor above this one,' he continued. 'Would you like to see that as well?'

He led the way up to the small rooms under the steep roof. They were as charming as the larger rooms on the floors below.

'What do you use them for?' Maggy enquired.

He shrugged. 'An overflow of guests. At one time the servants slept here, but Anny has a small flat downstairs; and the other servants don't sleep in the house.'

They went downstairs slowly, stopping to look at portraits and paintings as they went. On the first floor Maggy stopped before the painting of a girl with eyes and hair done in the style of the mid-eighteenth century.

'She's not Dutch, I think?'

'No—she was the bride of the Doelsma who built this house; she came from Scotland to marry him and because she hadn't been to Holland before he had the furniture in her bedroom sent from England, so that she shouldn't feel strange. There's a family tradition that no bride may see the room until she comes to this house after her marriage.'

Maggy studied the pretty face in the portrait. 'He must have loved her very much,' she said at last.

He smiled. 'Yes, indeed, as she loved him. They

had nine children, all of whom survived—a miracle
for those days, was it not?' He turned down a short
passage and switched on a light. 'Here they are—the
whole family.' He pointed to a small canvas.

'You look exactly like him,' Maggy cried—as indeed he did.

'Yes, I know, but whether I follow his excellent
example and have nine children is still a matter for
conjecture.' He was laughing as he switched off the
light and led the way downstairs.

As they entered the drawing room, Mevrouw
Doelsma looked up.

'Well, my dear, what do you think of the house?'

'It's beautiful, Mevrouw Doelsma. I haven't any
words to say how beautiful. Thank you for waiting
so patiently for me. I expect you would like to go
upstairs and rest for an hour. I'll read to you if you
like—you'll enjoy the evening more if you lie down
for a wee while.'

Dinner was a pleasant meal. Maggy still found a
secret delight in the delicious food, even more delicious when eaten off Meissen plates with silver
knives and forks.

The hospital appointment was for ten o'clock the
following morning and was thoroughly discussed.
They were to be driven to the nearby hospital by
Pratt, who would then return to Oudehof.

'I shall go to bed early,' declared Mevrouw
Doelsma, 'for I have no intention of anybody finding
anything wrong with me tomorrow.' Accordingly,

soon after dinner, she said goodnight to Paul, but
when Maggy wished him goodnight too, he said,

'Come downstairs again, Maggy, when Mother is
safely in bed, and I'll take you on a tour of the salon.'

His mother paused on her way upstairs. 'What a
good idea, Paul! Maggy, it's only just after nine, you
can't possibly go to bed yet.'

Maggy agreed; indeed, it would have been difficult
for her to do otherwise, and her inclination to spend
an hour in Paul's company was very strong.

It was an hour or more before she went quietly into
the drawing room. As the doctor got up from his chair
she said rather breathlessly,

'I'm sorry I have been so long. Your mother is
excited, I couldna' leave her. She's douce the noo'.
I've kept ye out of bed.'

The doctor looked astonished. 'I seldom go upstairs
before midnight and very often later; being solitary,
I'm afraid I have acquired bad habits.' His grey eyes
twinkled at her, and she smiled shyly, supposing he
thought her foolish, but there was no mockery in his
gaze; he was looking at her kindly with no trace of
his usual slightly arrogant expression. He crossed the
room and stood beside her.

'Shall we start on this side first?' he queried mildly.

They lingered a long time over the china and silver
and the numerous paintings on the walls. Some of
them, he told her, had been in the family for many
years. They pored over a small Cornelis Troost and a
skating scene by Avercamp, and at length came back
to the big stove where he pulled the bell rope. When

Anny came, Paul said, 'You'd like a cup of coffee, wouldn't you, Maggy?'

She was absorbed in the tiles around the stove. 'Aye, Doctor, coffee will suit me fine. I canna' understand this wee tile.' She pointed to it, set high in the wall behind the stove. It had a design of ships and sheep and a disembodied hand holding a sword aloft, the whole encircled by an inscription impossible for her to read.

He came and stood beside her. 'That's the family crest; the ships and the sheep from which we made our living—the sword is a polite indication that we are prepared to fight for what we have.' He traced the writing with a long forefinger, and spelled it out in the Friesian tongue. 'I honour God, and love that which is mine.'

Maggy turned to look at him. 'And you do, don't you?' she asked.

His grey eyes smiled down into her brown ones.

'Yes, Maggy, I do.' He bent his head and kissed her on one soft cheek.

'Oh!' said Maggy, and said no more, for Anny had opened the door and was coming in with the coffee tray. The doctor laughed softly and said, 'Do pour out, Maggy.'

She did so, with commendable calm, and even maintained her share of conversation while they drank it, and then wished the doctor a quiet goodnight before going upstairs to her pretty bedroom, to lie awake in the canopied bed, her usual good sense wholly at war with her unbidden thoughts.

CHAPTER SIX

THERE WAS NO SIGN of Dr Doelsma when Maggy and Mevrouw Doelsma arrived at the hospital the following morning. Instead they were met by a comfortable middle-aged Sister, who bore them off to the X-ray department. Maggy looked around her with professional interest, oblivious of the equally interested glances she received as they walked through the corridors. The cubicle they were shown into was small and white-painted, and smelled, inevitably, of hospital. It looked exactly the same as those in her own hospital. She helped her patient to undress, and persuaded her to put on the shapeless white cotton garment, tied with tapes at the back. Dr Doelsma had told them that an ECG would be done first, before the X-ray examination, and Maggy made her patient as comfortable as possible on the narrow couch, keeping up a calming flow of small talk meanwhile. Mevrouw Doelsma was nervous, but Maggy knew that they wouldn't have to wait. There were, she thought dryly, many advantages in being a relative of a hospital consultant. The ECG technician proved to be a white-overalled girl, pretty and competent. Between them she and Maggy made tight work of the tiresome straps and buckles criss-crossed over Mevrouw Doelsma's unwilling body. Ten minutes later she was sitting up once more, asking rather querulously how much longer she had to wear the shapeless white garment.

'A wee while, yet, Mevrouw Doelsma,' said Maggy soothingly. 'I've your dressing gown and slippers here.' This act of thoughtfulness had quite a cheering effect as they were conducted to the consultant's room. Maggy had expected to remain outside while Dr Bennink examined Mevrouw Doelsma, but was bidden to stay by Dr Bennink, who was obviously good friends with his patient. He was a short, rather stout man, with grey hair receding from a high forehead; he wore very thick glasses and peered at Maggy through them rather like an earnest little boy looking through the end of a bottle. He beamed at her, lowered the glasses to have a better look, and then shook hands, and such was his personality that she was unaware that she towered over him by more than eight inches.

'*Kijk maar*—the Scottish Sister. I know of you, naturally. I am now happy to be acquainted.' He waved her to a seat by Mevrouw Doelsma and took his own chair again.

Dr Bennink had undoubtedly earned his reputation as a leading heart consultant. His questions were searching and he was very thorough. Maggy came in for her fair share and answered him with an unflurried accuracy which pleased him mightily. He liked the way she did everything necessary during the ensuing examination too. She appeared to read his wishes before they were voiced and acted upon them before he uttered them. After half an hour, he sat back. 'You're as good as new, Henrietta, due doubtless to your stubbornness and this young woman. I'll see Paul after your barium meal. With a regular check-up and sensible living, you'll outlive the lot of us.'

His myopic eyes twinkled as they all shook hands, and a cheerful buxom little nurse with a round face and bright blue eyes took charge of them once more. Back in the cubicle, she produced a tumbler of thick white fluid and gave it to Maggy. Maggy in her turn proffered it to her patient, who obediently took a sip, and immediately declared her intention of not drinking any more of it.

'It's revolting!' she said indignantly.

'Yes, I know,' said Maggy, 'but it will be impossible to carry out the tests unless you drink it,' she added reasonably.

'Then I won't have the tests,' said Mevrouw Doelsma testily.

'Paul wanted you to have them.' Maggy no sooner uttered the words than she blushed; she always thought of the doctor as Paul, but that was no excuse. She could have bitten her thoughtless tongue. Fortunately Mevrouw Doelsma hadn't seemed to have noticed her words, but was busy pulling a loose thread on her despised gown. Maggy proffered the glass once more, and was surprised when the nauseating liquid was swallowed without further fuss, and she was able to lead a surprisingly docile patient into the X-ray room.

Excepting for a dim red light, the place was in

darkness. Mevrouw Doelsma clutched Maggy's hand and jumped when a vague figure loomed before them. It spoke in a reassuringly human voice, albeit in Dutch; However, it sounded soothing and friendly, and Mevrouw Doelsma answered it with every sign of pleasure. The voice changed to a pedantic and nearly perfect English.

'How do you do, Sister. Paul has told me of you, and I am happy to see you.'

Maggy said politely. 'How do you do?' wondering if the figure could see her any better than she could see him. He went on to give a few brisk instructions, which Maggy carried out before stepping backwards against the wall, out of the way. A slight sound and a draught behind her made her realise that she was standing in front of a door. Before she could move, a vast arm was dropped lightly about her shoulders.

'Hallo, Maggy,' said the doctor very softly; she felt his breath on her cheek, and fought to keep her own breath steady, trying to ignore the rush of feeling at his touch. He remained where he was for a long minute, then gave her shoulder a friendly squeeze and went silently through the gloom to the radiographer. They murmured together until Paul said, 'Hallo, Mother. We shan't be long now.'

His mother's voice sounded faintly querulous. 'It's so dark, Paul, and I don't know where Maggy is.'

'She's quite close, dear, but she must keep out of the way for a moment. She'll stand by you presently while we screen your tummy. Now do what Dirk says, Mama.'

The lights went on again, Mevrouw Doelsma was arranged as comfortably as possible on the table, and Maggy, protected by a lead apron, stood beside her, holding her hand. The dark was intense this time, with only the greenish, dim flicker of the screen. Maggy listened to the two men making their observations in low voices, and gave the small clutching hand she was holding a reassuring squeeze. It seemed a long time before the lights went on again and she led her patient back to the cubicle and helped her dress. Both doctors were waiting for them; it was the radiologist who spoke.

'Mevrouw Doelsma, as far as I can see there's nothing at all for you to worry about. I'll have to check the X-rays, of course, but neither Paul nor I could see anything amiss. So you need have no fear of complications. Dr Bennink will be seeing you shortly again, I expect. I must congratulate you on an excellent recovery.'

There was delicious hot coffee waiting for them in the doctor's office, where they were joined by Dr Bennick. Maggy sat quietly, saying almost nothing, and feeling uncomfortable. Her presence meant that the other three must speak English. She was sure that they must have a great deal to talk about—the intimate gossip of old friends, perhaps; family matters in which she had no part. She struggled to think of an excuse so that she could leave them. She put her coffee cup down on the desk beside her, and as though it were a signal, the doctor got up and came over to her.

'I'd like to take you round part of the hospital. Are you ready, Maggy?'

He didn't wait for an answer, but opened the door, calling a casual *'dag'* over his shoulder at his mother and Dr Bennink as he stood waiting for Maggy to join him.

They walked along a number of rather bleak corridors, and she, feeling that anything was better than silence, plunged into a series of questions which the doctor answered patiently, pausing only to acknowledge gravely any greetings he received from passing doctors and students. They went first, and inevitably, to the women's medical ward. Maggy was surprised and faintly amused to see that the nurses held the doctor in some awe. Even the Ward Sister, a gaunt, elderly woman with a sweet face, seemed stiff and formal with him. They walked round the ward, the two women comparing notes with the doctor acting as interpreter, and then sat in Sister's office drinking another cup of coffee, telling each other about salaries and off-duty and lack of nurses, and stopped reluctantly when the doctor remarked mildly that he thought it a good idea if they went to see the children's ward. Here everything was noise and bustle and small children shouting and crying and laughing, according to how they felt. The doctor seemed to know them all as they wandered through the ward to the balcony, accompanied by Sister, a pretty young creature who quite obviously loved her work.

'There's a child I want you to see, Maggy. She's making a remarkable recovery after eating coal,

safety-pins, a few small coins and a large lump of
Plasticine. She's Sister's pet, isn't she, Sister?' He
turned to the Ward Sister and said something in Dutch
to make her laugh; she was still laughing when she
went back into the ward, leaving them looking at the
small blonde angel playing with a doll on the floor.
She eyed them for a moment, then threw the doll
away and got on to rather spindly little legs and tod-
dled over to Maggy, who bent and swung her up to
be cuddled.

'You clever girl,' said Maggy, dropping a kiss on
the straight hair. She looked at Paul. 'Isn't she beautiful, Doctor?'

'The most beautiful girl in the world.' But he
wasn't looking at his small patient. He bent forward,
and Maggy felt his lips on hers. She stood quite still,
looking at him, her cheeks very pink, but her brown
eyes met his grey ones squarely.

'I don't intend to apologise, Maggy,' he said, almost lazily.

Maggy forced her voice to normality. 'There is no
need, Doctor. I doubt ye've kissed many a girl before
me, and will kiss many more. I ken well it means
nothing to ye.' She gave the toddler a reassuring hug,
and put her back on the rug on the floor.

'Just a minute, Maggy. Are you so sure of that?'

She looked over her shoulder at him; he was standing with his hands in his pockets, looking at her with
a faint mocking smile on his face.

'Aye,' she said slowly. 'I'm sure. A kiss can mean
everything in this world to two people, and it can be

just an empty gesture, like saying "How do you do" and not wanting to know.' She bent down and gave the little girl her doll, then went on, 'Ye must be proud of the bairn, in a few weeks she'll be a bonny wee lassie.'

She blew kisses to the small creature, and went back into the ward without looking at him. They said goodbye to the Sister and started on their way back to his office. Maggy kept up a steady flow of small talk, scarcely waiting for his replies before plunging into a fresh topic; walking just ahead of him, so that she didn't need to look at him. When they reached the office door, she put her hand on the knob and faced him. She had forced a cheerful expression on to her face, but her eyes looked like a small girl's when she'd been hurt.

'Thank you for showing me round, Dr Doelsma. It was most interesting.'

He put a large hand over hers, so that she was unable to turn the knob.

'My poor Maggy,' he said. 'You may be six feet tall, but you've not grown up yet.'

He opened the door then, and Maggy went inside, and waited while Mevrouw Doelsma made her fare-wells, then said goodbye quietly herself, before going out to the car and back to the Rapoenburg and the doctor's house. As they entered the hall, Mevrouw Doelsma said, 'Paul will be home for lunch. I expect. What a pity the weather is so bad, Maggy—it's no day for sightseeing.' She started up the stairs, with Maggy beside her. 'Never mind, I daresay it will be better tomorrow. We're staying a few days, anyway, and you shall have two or three days quite free to go sightseeing. We'll talk about it later, shall we?' She paused as the phone rang, and waited while Anny answered it.

'It's Mr Paul, madam, he asks me to tell you that he will be going to Utrecht almost immediately, and will lunch there. He expects to be home for dinner.'

Mevrouw Doelsma said nothing, but that evening, when she and Maggy went downstairs to the salon and found Paul waiting, she remarked rather tartly,

'Paul, I know the love of your life is in Utrecht, but did you really have to go this morning? I know you like to go as often as possible, but surely, when we are here…?'

He was pouring drinks at a side table and turned a suddenly forbidding face to her.

'I'm sorry, Mother, but it is important to me, and there is no point in discussing it, is there?' He walked across the room and gave her the small glass of sherry she was allowed, then bent his great height and kissed her cheek. He was smiling again. 'I had no idea that I would be going to Utrecht until I rang up, Mama. Am I forgiven?'

He turned away to get a drink for Maggy, and drew her into a conversation he deliberately made light.

Maggy had spent a wretched afternoon; it seemed obvious to her that Paul, however good his opinion was of her as a nurse, had none at all of her as a woman. She sipped some sherry. How could she have thought even for one moment that he had any interest in her whatsoever? He was quite right, she hadn't grown up. But now, she told herself firmly, she had very positive proof; Stien lived in Utrecht—the love of his life. Mevrouw Doelsma had said.

Her good Scottish pride came to her rescue. She drank the rest of her sherry in time to answer a question from the doctor in a perfectly natural and friendly voice.

Dinner was a gay meal; they drank champagne to celebrate Mevrouw Doelsma's recovery, and sat round the table talking long after the meal was finished.

'Maggy's having a day off in a couple of days' time,' said Mevrouw Doelsma.

Paul glanced briefly at the serene profile; Maggy had contrived not to look at him, save for a fleeting glance when she spoke to him. She didn't look now.

'Where are you going?'

'Amsterdam,' she replied promptly. 'I want to see the museums and churches first, and the Dam Palace, and tour the canals, and look at the shops...'

Her companions laughed. 'Why, Maggy,' said Mevrouw Doelsma, 'you'll be worn out. You must have another day...'

'Then I shall go again and just walk around, looking.'

The doctor leaned back in his chair. 'There is a great deal to see, but may I suggest that you keep to the main streets—it's easy to get lost unless you know the city, especially if you intend to roam. I've a map you shall have—there are one or two areas I should avoid if I were you. The Jordaan, picturesque and harmless enough, but if you got lost there I doubt if they would understand you, and you certainly wouldn't understand them.' He paused. 'There are one or two other districts you should avoid.'

Maggy looked at him with brows raised. 'But, Doctor,' she said mildly, 'I'm six feet tall, but for a quarter of an inch, and well used to managing for myself.'

A corner of the doctor's mouth twitched. 'The particular district I have in mind is behind the Oude Kerk, which I imagine is one of the churches you wish to see. We call it the Rossebuurt. The—er—ladies of the town ply their trade there.' He added gently, 'They'd do you no harm, but you would be out of your element, wouldn't you?'

Maggy could think of nothing to say in answer to this, but sat, staring at him, and going slowly very red. Mevrouw Doelsma came to her rescue. 'Paul, you're making Maggy blush; be quiet! Give the child your map and mark off the less inviting areas and then she'll know what to avoid.' She got up. 'Now I'm going up to bed; I've had an exciting day.'

Accompanied by Maggy, she crossed the lovely room and the hall and started up the stairs. The doctor had come with them; now he kissed his mother and turned to Maggy.

'When Mother is safely in bed, will you come down again and I will give you the map.'

Maggy took a step up the stairs, away from him. 'Perhaps you would leave it somewhere?' She glanced around her. 'On one of the tables here perhaps?' She took another step. 'I'm rather tired, Doctor. I think I shall go to my room when I've put Mevrouw Doelsma to bed.'

'It would be better if I showed you the map—if you are too tired to come down, I'll come up to your room presently, shall I?' He looked at his watch. 'Half an hour—forty minutes?' He was laughing at her.

Maggy quelled him with a severe glance. 'I'll be down in half an hour or so, Doctor,' she said soberly, and went upstairs without another word.

It was almost an hour later when she knocked on the library door and went inside. The doctor got up from his desk and came over to her, for she had made no effort to go into the room. He held the map in his hand. 'You'll have to come over to the desk, I think, so that I can spread it out.'

She went rather reluctantly to stand beside him while he pointed out the areas he had ringed and the neat list of train and bus times he had written in one corner.

'I don't like you going alone, Maggy, but I have no right or reason to ask you not to. Will you ring up either the hospital or here if you want to be fetched. The phone numbers are here.'

Maggy took the map from him. 'It's a great trouble ye've taken, Doctor, and I'm grateful.'

'I am, after all, responsible for you while you are under my roof, my dear girl, and it's very little I'm doing.'

She turned to the door, and he made no attempt to stop her.

'Thank you. Doctor, I'll away to my bed.'

She was at the door when he spoke. 'Still friends, Maggy?'

She turned and gave him a steady look. 'Aye, Doctor, still friends.'

Maggy went down to her breakfast the next morning, wondering if she would see the doctor. There was no sign of him, however, although when she returned to her patient, who had breakfasted in bed, it was to hear that he had been in to see his mother while Maggy was at her own breakfast. There was very little nursing treatment to be done, and later, when Mevrouw Doelsma was dressed and she was standing looking out of the window, she said suddenly,

'We will go for a little run in the car—Paul has arranged for Pratt to stay on for a few days.' She seemed delighted with the idea, and Maggy agreed readily—it was a pleasant enough day, and it would be nice to see something of the country around Leiden. Pratt installed them both comfortably in the back of the car, and asked, 'A little drive to the villa, perhaps, madam?'

'An excellent idea, Pratt, and keep off the main roads, won't you?' Pratt agreed gravely to this request, and took them through the peaceful, quiet countryside; he drove at considerably less speed than did the doctor, and it took them an hour or more to reach the village of Loenen, where, it seemed, Mevrouw Doelsma wished to go. It was an enchanting spot, on the banks of the River Vecht. They left the village and travelled along the road running beside the river; on both banks there were charming, rather ornate villas. Maggy found them rather too elaborate—they reminded her of birthday cakes—but there was no denying their charm, or the beauty of their surroundings.

Pratt slowed down and turned into an unpretentious gateway leading to one of the smaller and less ornate of the houses. Maggy caught a glimpse of the river at the back of the garden as he drew up before its solid front door. They got out, assisted in a fatherly fashion by Pratt. 'We'll have coffee here,' said Mevrouw Doelsma, as he rang the bell. The door was opened by a short, stout, elderly woman in a blue striped dress and white apron, who broke immediately into speech.

'Madam dear! Come in—I said to myself today, Madam will be here any day now; and so I told Mijnheer.' She paused for breath and embraced Mevrouw Doelsma, then stood back and looked at her. 'You look wonderful, madam, and how's my boy? I haven't seen him for weeks.'

Mevrouw Doelsma took this torrent of speech calmly. 'Mr Paul is a busy man, as you know, Nanny.' She turned to Maggy, standing patiently beside her. 'Maggy, you must meet Nanny. She looked after Paul and Saskia and Wiebecka, and now she lives here and looks after my brother-in-law.'

Maggy proffered a hand, and shook the small plump one offered to her carefully, taking care not to squeeze the elderly fingers with her own strong large ones. Nanny looked her up and down, and she stood quietly waiting for the sharp blue eyes to have their fill.

'There's a big girl now,' said Nanny comfortably. 'Not far short of Master Paul, I daresay.'

She led the way indoors through an elegant small hall into the living room, and went to fetch the master of the house.

He was, even at seventy, very like Paul. He had the same grey eyes and straight nose, and the same air of arrogance. He greeted them with delight, and openly looked Maggy over as they drank their coffee.

'You're a fine girl,' he said with the outspokenness of the elderly. 'I like an Amazon myself—just as Paul does—or perhaps he hasn't told you that,' he added slyly.

Maggy blushed, but answered coolly enough, 'No, I don't believe he has.'

'You can colour up too,' he went on relentlessly. 'Haven't seen a girl blush for years—didn't know they could any more.' He put on a pair of old-fashioned spectacles and peered at her. 'Has Paul seen you blush?'

Maggy put down her coffee cup carefully.

'Very probably—it's an unfortunate habit I haven't been able to stop.'

She was scarlet by now, and decided that he was quite the most impossible old gentleman she had met. She was horrified when he answered her unspoken thought.

'I'm a rude old man, aren't I?' He spoke with satisfaction in his careful English. He added obscurely, 'I'm fond of Paul.'

Maggy replied politely that she supposed he was, and he smiled at her, looking so like Paul that she smiled back. 'Delightful,' he murmured, and then out loud. 'Go and have a look at the garden, you'll be glad of a breath of air. You're too young to be cooped up indoors.'

Maggy got up obediently and went outside and walked around the small paths between the flower beds, and down to the river, where she sat down to admire the view on a seat thoughtfully provided for just that purpose. She supposed she could stay for half an hour or so. Mevrouw Doelsma would want to talk for a little while. She decided that she liked Paul's uncle despite his forthright manner; she wished she knew more about him. Her thoughts were interrupted by Nanny, who had appeared silently beside her and offered to keep her company. Maggy made room for her on the seat, and spent the next ten minutes asking questions about the river and the fairy-tale houses bordering it. Nanny replied to her questions at some length, so that Maggy not only heard about the houses but the people who lived in them as well.

When she at length paused to draw breath, Maggy asked. 'Have you lived here long, and may I know your name? I don't feel that I should call you Nanny.'

'The name's Coffin—a good West Country name, miss. I came to Holland with Madam when she married and I've been here ever since. The master sent us to England, but Master Paul, he wouldn't go—

stayed with his father. Not eight he wasn't, but very determined. He was a fine boy, and grown to a fine man. Very naughty he was when he was a little boy.'

It was obvious to her listener that Nanny adored him. 'That makes two of us,' thought Maggy wistfully. She listened to the old lady reliving her busy, happy past, until, in the middle of an involved story about Paul's eventful childhood, she broke off.

'There, miss, you won't want to hear all this…?'

Maggy answered without thinking. 'Oh, but I do! Please go on—I'm so very interested.' She was watching the river as she spoke, and didn't see Nanny's beady eyes studying her face. Nanny said nothing, but finished her story, and then said surprisingly,

'I'd be happy for you to call me Nanny, miss.'

Maggy realised that Nanny was bestowing a favour, not lightly given. She answered gravely, 'Thank you, Miss Coffin. I should like to call you Nanny.'

Nanny nodded her head. 'I have the second sight,' she said obscurely, and plunged back into the past, sure of her audience.

Mevrouw Doelsma and Maggy, being driven back to Leiden by the sedate Pratt, had plenty to talk about; at least, Mevrouw Doelsma chattered happily about the visit.

'Did you like Mijnheer Doelsma, Maggy?' she asked.

'Aye. Mevrouw Doelsma, I did—he and the doctor are very like.'

'Yes, indeed. They're fond of each other too. It's Paul's house, you know, but he gave it to his uncle to live in until his death, and it's so convenient that Nanny is there to keep house for him—Isn't Nanny wonderful?'

Maggy agreed. 'I didn't know there were nannies like her—I mean outside books.'

'She's never changed since she first came to me; that's—let me see. Paul's thirty-six—it must be all of thirty-seven years. She went and looked after Saskia's and Wiebecka's babies when they were born, but she wouldn't stay with them—said she had to be free to look after Paul's children when he marries.'

That was the second time in twenty-four hours that Paul's marriage had been mentioned. Maggy watched the half-formed wisps of her dreams dissolve into a bleak future, then turned her attention to the countryside, asking sensible, observant questions of her patient which kept that lady fully occupied until they reached the doctor's house once more.

They ate a leisurely lunch, and having seen Mevrouw Doelsma tucked up for her afternoon nap, Maggy donned a raincoat, tied a scarf under her chin against the threatening rain, and set off to explore. Pratt, appearing in a silent, magic sort of way, opened the front door and hoped that she would enjoy her walk. She smiled at him, went down the double steps to the pavement, and started walking along the Rapenburg. The houses which lined the canal were beautiful, some very old, some not so old, but all making a harmonious whole. She didn't hurry, but looked at each house as she passed it. She turned back from the contemplation of a particularly fine fanlight, to find the Rolls loitering to a gentle halt beside her; the top was down, and Dr Doelsma, apparently impervious to the chilly wind blowing along the canal, was sitting at the wheel. He waved a languid hand, elegantly gloved.

'Good afternoon, Maggy. Off duty?'

She nodded, looking cross because she was blushing for no reason at all, and because she was wearing her serviceable raincoat and had her hair tied up anyhow in the first scarf she could find. His glance flickered over her, and he said,

'Don't worry, Maggy, you look delightful.'

Her brows met in a thunderous frown, and an explosive, 'Och!' burst from her lips, but before she could answer, he had waved again and slid quietly away. By concentrating hard on the houses she was passing, she managed not to think of him at all, as she made her way to Noordeind, where she turned back and started to walk back on the other side of the canal. There was a nice old house on the corner which had been turned into a restaurant, and she stopped to look at it. The interior was discreetly veiled from the vulgar eye of the passer-by, but it looked expensive. She stood in front of the door, wondering what it would be like inside, and heard nothing at all until the doctor spoke just behind her.

'Ah! As usual, Sister MacFergus is in the right place at the right time.'

Before she could turn her head, she was guided by

an inescapable hand on her elbow through the door. It was another Dutch interior—very old, very quaint and quiet. She sat down, speechlessly obedient, at the small table to which he had guided her, while he ordered tea. He sat down opposite her, the frail chair creaking alarmingly under his weight.

'And what have you done today, Maggy?'

She undid her head-scarf with fingers which shook slightly, willing her voice to normality.

'Mevrouw Doelsma took me to visit your uncle at Loenen.'

'Uncle Cornelis?' He laughed softly. 'Was he outrageous? I'm sure he made you blush, Maggy—' he watched her across the table. 'Yes, I see he did.'

She looked down her exquisite nose at him.

'Your uncle is—is very nice. I like him.'

'I'm sure he liked you too. He has a passion for large women.'

She went scarlet under his amused gaze, and said haughtily,

'I'm aware, Doctor. He told me so—' She remembered what else he had said, and looked down at her plate, so that her black lashes lay on her cheeks, wishing to be anywhere but where she was.

'Did he tell you that I have a passion for big women too?'

She refused to look up, and after a moment he said with a laugh in his voice, 'Poor Maggy, I mustn't tease.'

The tea came, and with it the return of her composure. The doctor maintained an easy flow of small talk, and as always in his company, she found herself responding to his friendliness.

She passed him his tea, and watched while he helped himself lavishly to sugar, then turned to choose a monumental confection of chocolate and whipped cream and pineapple from the proffered tray. She eyed it with healthy pleasure, and attacked it with the endearing enthusiasm of a small girl having an unexpected treat. The doctor chose *boterkoek* and asked,

'Did you see Nanny?'

'Yes, she came and sat with me in the garden and told me tales of when you were a little boy. You were naughty, weren't you?' she added severely.

'Oh dear! Not the one about the Ambassador's wig?'

She nodded. 'Yes, Dr Doelsma, and the frog in your Great-Aunt Wilhelmina's bed, and skating instead of going to school…'

He held up a large hand. 'Enough! Maggy, I'm on my knees. Nanny has been devastatingly plainspoken, as always.' He passed his tea cup for more tea. 'Did you like the villa?'

'Aye, Doctor, such a dear wee place, and the beautiful garden and the river close by.'

He nodded. 'Yes, it's pretty enough—just right for my uncle. Nanny finds it quiet; she has an insatiable passion for babies and small children.'

Just for a moment Maggy glimpsed a lovely impossible dream, then said in a bright voice,

'She looks just as a nanny should look. She's very fond of you, isn't she?'

'I believe so, though I can't think why. I must have been a great trial to her. She seems to have—er—unburdened herself to you.'

Maggy looked surprised. 'Did she? She asked me to call her Nanny,' she added.

He raised his eyebrows. 'Did she indeed? That's unusual. She's more fiercely family than we are, you know. I've never known her do that before.'

Maggy agreed. 'I realised that. I felt honoured. She told me about her second sight too.'

The doctor gave her a long stare across the table, and said nothing, watching Maggy tie on her scarf again.

'Thank you for my tea, Doctor, and I'll be on my way.'

Outside it was raining in earnest and the wind was coming and going in spiteful little gusts. The doctor took her arm and said,

'It won't take any longer to walk this way—I'll show you the University. We can cross the bridge there and walk back on the other side.'

They stepped out briskly, not saying much until they reached the old building. 'Did you study here, Doctor?' Maggy asked.

'Yes—it's the oldest university in Holland, you know, and we're all rather proud of it. I was at Cambridge too, and Edinburgh Royal, but I came back here.'

They walked on, more slowly.

'Do you like Leiden?' he asked.

'Very much, so far. The Rapenburg is beautiful. Do you prefer it to Oudehof?'

They crossed the bridge, she could see his home now, and the Rolls-Royce standing outside.

'What a difficult question to answer. I think I like them both equally.'

They reached the house, and he went up the steps with her, pulled the old-fashioned bell, and waited until Anny opened the door. He didn't go in, but said,

'Goodbye, Maggy. Will you make my excuses to my mother? I'm going over to Utrecht and shan't be back until late. Have a good day in Amsterdam if I don't see you again.'

He sounded casual. Maggy answered him quietly and went through the door and up the stairs to her room, where she stood before the mirror looking at herself. He had said 'You look delightful,' but he hadn't meant it, of course. Slow tears started to trickle down her cheeks. He would be on his way to Utrecht now—on his way to Stien. She tore off her coat and scarf and washed her face and changed into uniform again, and went, with a cheerful face, to deliver Paul's message to his mother.

CHAPTER SEVEN

MAGGY LEFT the house quite early the next morning
making sure before she went that Mevrouw
Doelsma's gently patterned day should run smoothly.
She sat in the train, wondering whether she should
make the suggestion that there was really no further
need of her services. She got out at Amsterdam with
the question still unsolved, and then forgot all about
it in the excitement of being in a strange city in a
strange land, and with all day before her to explore
it.

It seemed logic to take a canal trip straight away—
there was a launch standing beside its own small pier
just across the street. Maggy crossed cautiously,
bought her ticket and spent the next hour or so looking at Amsterdam from the water. She didn't listen to
the guide, saying everything three times in three lan-
guages; she didn't care about the names of the old
buildings they passed, or who owned them, but just
sat quietly, looking about her; she would go for a
second time on her next free day, and behave like a
tourist.

Back on the Damrak, she took out her map and
studied it carefully, then made her way to the Palace
and the War Memorial in the Dam Square; she studied them both at length, then strolled down the Kal-

verstraat, looking at the shops—they were inviting
and expensive. Maggy studied the gay autumn colours. It would be nice to buy anything one fancied
without having to worry if it would wear well or look
fashionable in a year's time. She glanced down at her
own dress, a navy blue and white checked tricot, well
cut but not, she realised, spectacular. There was a
vivid coral pink jersey dress in one window, very
plain, very well cut. It had no price tag. Maggy went
inside, and speaking good clear Scots, asked to see it.
The price was high, but as the saleswoman assured
her, it was exactly the right dress for her. Looking at
herself in the long, elegant mirror in the small fitting
room, Maggy had to agree. It was a beautiful dress.
She paid for it quickly before her practical mind told
her that she was being extravagant, and left the shop
happily.

She lunched at the Formosa Café, because the doctor had told her to do so, and ate her way through a
twaalf, studying her map. The Rijksmuseum was easy
to find, but after half an hour she decided that she
was doing the magnificent paintings less than justice
by offering them the glance that was all the time she
had for them. She wanted to sit and look at them in
her own good time. She would most certainly have to
return on the second free day Mevrouw Doelsma had
promised her.

She walked back towards the centre of the city,
getting happily lost, and spending far too long peering
into the antique shops in the narrow streets lining the
canals. Eventually she found her way back to the Kal-

verstraat, and because she couldn't find a tea-shop, ventured rather shyly into the Hotel Polen, where a fatherly waiter gave her tea, straw-coloured and very weak, and dish of delightful cakes. The day had passed very quickly. Maggy looked at her watch and decided that she would just have time to visit the Scottish Church before she went back to the station. It was easy enough to find, and surprisingly peaceful, standing in the little square of old houses, with the bustle of the city all round it. She left it reluctantly, and found her way back to the Dam Square; and because she had a little time to spare plunged into the Nieuwendijk. According to the map, the station would be at the other end, and it looked interesting, with a great many shops each side of a very narrow street, there was a strip of pavement on either side of the cobblestones, and Maggy walked briskly, resisting the temptation to stop and look in the shop windows; she wasn't sure how far away the station was.

There were a great many people about; she was pushed and jostled and bumped into, but all with the greatest good humour, and after a time she hardly noticed it until a small woman, darting out of a narrow alley, knocked against her and would have fallen if Maggy hadn't caught her by the shoulder. Their surprise was mutual—it was Madame Riveau. Maggy recognised her at once, and Madame Riveau knew her too. She was very pale, her black eyes blank with what might have been pain. Maggy blinked with astonishment. The woman looked far worse than she had ever looked at St Ethelburga's. She said gently, remembering to speak French,

'Are you hurt, Madame Riveau? You are so white.'

The woman shook her head, staring at Maggy as though she could not believe her eyes.

'You're not well?' Maggy went on. This time Madame Riveau mumbled, 'Yes, yes, Sister.' Maggy, puzzled at her strange behaviour, tried again.

'Do you live near here?'

Her companion nodded again, and this time nodded reluctantly, displaying toothless gums.

'So you've had your teeth out,' said Maggy, glad of something to talk about to this awkward woman. 'Do you remember that I said you should do so?' She remembered how unpleasant the men had been about it. 'Was your husband angry?' She saw fear flicker in the woman's eyes. 'Does he take you to the doctor?'

Madame Riveau went even whiter. So that was it! She said, 'Sister, come again, I must see you. Why are you here?'

'I came to Holland to work,' Maggy said briefly. She saw no reason to tell the woman more—besides, her vocabulary was being stretched to its limits. She held out her hand, but surprisingly Madame Riveau became all of a sudden quite friendly.

'Do you often come to Amsterdam, Sister?'

'No, I don't,' said Maggy, 'but I shall be here again tomorrow or the next day.'

Madame Riveau was still holding her hand. 'I should like to see you and talk—I am not well, you saw that, did you not? I live near here. Perhaps if you come again, about this time—just for a few minutes.'

Maggy gently withdrew her hand; the woman certainly looked ill, and after all she wasn't a stranger. She nodded reluctantly. 'I may come, but I can't promise,' she said.

Madame Riveau smiled her horrible toothless smile. 'Good, good, I shall count on you. *Au revoir,* Sister.'

She disappeared into the crowd of people milling around them on the narrow pavement, and Maggy, mindful of her train, quickened her steps to the station.

When she got back to the doctor's house, she was fully occupied with Mevrouw Doelsma until dinner time. The doctor joined them in the dining room, but it wasn't until half way through the meal that he asked Maggy casually if she had enjoyed her day. She answered briefly, afraid that it would bore him to have a detailed account of her comings and goings. He listened courteously, but didn't press her for details, and presently began to talk about plans for his mother's proposed holiday later on—it seemed that he owned a villa in the south of France as well. She supposed he was quite rich, and the thought depressed her.

Maggy turned to answer a question from Mevrouw Doelsma; she wasn't wearing uniform but had put on a sleeveless dress in a pink patterned silky material; its simple lines accentuated her delightful figure, the colour suited her clear skin and brown hair. She felt the doctor's eyes on her and looked at him and smiled pleasantly and entirely without coquetry, and turned her attention back to his mother. Paul sat deep in thought, remembering what Nanny had said to him earlier that day. He became aware of Maggy's lilting voice saying something about meeting a woman she knew; he caught the name and asked,

'Do you mean that peculiar French woman with the gastric ulcer in your ward at St Ethelburga's?'

She half turned her head. 'Yes, Doctor, only she is a Belgian. Do you remember her too? She had a horrid husband and an ugly wee brute of a son—she ran out of an alley today and almost knocked me down. She looked so frightened at first, and then became quite friendly. I expect she was as surprised as I was.'

He was on the point of asking her where she had met the woman when Anny came in to tell him that he was wanted on the telephone, and presently he came back to say that he had to go out to a patient and they didn't see him again that evening.

The next day was cold and blustery. Mevrouw Doelsma's hairdresser came in the morning, and after lunch they drove to the Hague where Maggy accompanied her patient from shop to shop. Mevrouw Doelsma had a nice taste in dress and bought several things that caught her fancy, never once, to Maggy's astonishment, enquiring their price. There was no sign of the doctor when they got back at tea time, nor did he appear at dinner. Anny volunteered the information that her master had gone to Utrecht again, and didn't know when he would be back.

'He's always in Utrecht,' grumbled Mevrouw

Doelsma, 'but really I haven't the heart to say anything to him; after all, it is what he wants.'

Maggy murmured non-committally and looked at
the trifle on her plate, something to which she was
very partial, then found that she had no appetite for
it. She would have to go back to London as soon as
possible; she seemed incapable of controlling her
feelings any more. If she never saw Paul again, perhaps she would be able to forget him; the unlikeli-
hood of this was of no comfort to her. She swallowed
the lump in her throat, and before she could change
her treacherous mind, said, 'Mevrouw Doelsma,
you'll not be needing me much longer. I'll be sorry
to go, but I should return to hospital, you know.'

The little lady blinked at her across the beautifully
appointed table.

'Maggy! Go? But I shall miss you terribly. I know
I don't need you, but couldn't you stay another week
or so?' She looked at Maggy's face, and sighed. 'No,
I see you couldn't. But what will Paul say? Has he
mentioned it to you?'

Maggy shook her head without speaking. 'Well,'
said Mevrouw Doelsma, 'you can't go until the doctor
says so.'

'Doctor Bennink said that you were ready to return
to normal life, didn't he? And you are his patient.'

'Maggy, you sound as though you wanted to go.'

Maggy made haste to deny this and said hastily,
'No indeed, I've enjoyed every moment of my stay
in Holland—and Friesland,' she added, mindful of the
doctor's strong views, even though he wasn't there.

'There's a shortage of staff at St Ethelburga's, and I ought to go.'

Mevrouw Doelsma sighed for a second time. 'Yes, my dear. I understand, but I shall be very sorry to see you go. We'll tell Paul tomorrow. We shall be going back to Oudehof in a few days' time; you can return from there, can't you?'

Maggy thanked her gravely. 'I'll write to Matron...' she began, to be interrupted by Mevrouw Doelsma.

'And, Maggy, you must go to Amsterdam again tomorrow as you planned. Mijnheer Doelsma will be coming to lunch, and will be very cross to miss you—but you may not have another chance. Oh dear! I can't bear the thought of you going.'

Maggy smiled at her. She had become very fond of Paul's mother while she had been nursing her.

'Now that you can lead a usual life again, you won't miss me for long,' she consoled her. 'You'll be going on holiday soon, and visiting your daughters, and seeing all your friends again.'

She led the conversation back to more cheerful topics, and succeeded so well that by bedtime Mevrouw Doelsma was happy again.

Maggy went to her own room, determined not to think about the doctor. She got out her map and began to plan her visit for the next day. She must remember to go down the Nieuwendijk again, in case Madame Riveau was looking for her. Maggy hoped that she wouldn't be there, but she had promised to look out for her, and her dislike of the woman was no reason for breaking her word.

She put the map aside and got up from the little chintz-covered chair by the window, and started to walk restlessly about the charming room, her thoughts a muddle of bitter regret at leaving and the certainty that she was doing the only thing possible.

Her eye lighted on the cardboard box containing her new dress. What a terrible waste of money! Paul was unlikely to see her in it now—that, she was honest to admit to herself, was why she had bought it. She shook it out of its tissue paper wrappings, and tried it on, then stood looking at her reflection in the long mirror hanging on one wall. She wasn't a vain girl, but she could see that it was very becoming to her. She decided to wear it in the morning, and took it off and hung it carefully in the vast wardrobe, thinking how nice it would be if Paul were to come back from Utrecht before they left for Oudehof, but it was unlikely that he would return from Utrecht just to wish her goodbye.

It was still early when she finally got to bed, and she wasn't in the least sleepy. She had been down to the library earlier in the evening, and spent a little while choosing a book, and when she came across *The Wind in the Willows* with Paul's name written on the fly-leaf, in a careful large hand, with the date, she had taken it. She liked the story, but she had chosen it because it had belonged to him when he was a small boy. She lay in bed, turning the pages, and wondering what he had been like all those years ago, and after a little while she fell asleep.

The persistent, gentle tapping on the door roused her, she sat up in bed and looked at her watch—it was past one o'clock. Maggy reached for her dressing gown, ran barefooted to the door, and flung it open, the only thought in her mind the one that Mevrouw Doelsma had been taken ill. The doctor looked enormous in the dim light of the passage.

She clutched at an elegant coat sleeve. 'Your mother?' she asked breathlessly.

He answered coolly, 'Sleeping soundly. I'm sorry if I wakened you; your light was on— it's rather late, I wondered if there was anything wrong.'

Maggy became aware of her hand, still on his arm. She whipped it away as though the fine cloth had burned it.

'Wrong? With me? No; I fell asleep with the lamp still on. It was careless of me. I'm sorry, Doctor.' She sounded very polite. The doctor didn't move, and Maggy, aware of bare feet and a dressing gown bundled around her like a sack, put a tentative hand up to her hair, certain that she looked terrible. She would have liked to shut the door; the longing to put out her hand again and touch him was so great that she put her hands behind her back like a small girl, and stood looking at him wordlessly.

He stared down at her without expression, and said in the same cool voice, 'You'd better get some sleep, hadn't you? Goodnight.'

He turned on his heel and went quietly down the

passage to the front of the house, where his own room was, leaving her to go back to bed, to lie awake. He had wanted to be friends; Maggy wondered what had happened to change him; she went to sleep at last, still puzzling about it.

The weather was glorious when she set out the next morning, and she wore the new dress. There was the possibility of rain—there always was in Holland—so at the last minute she tucked the scarf she had worn when she had had tea with Paul into her handbag. The wind could be worse than the rain.

She spent the morning walking about the Singels, wishing she could see inside the lovely old houses which lined them, and then did some shopping for presents and had a leisurely lunch at the Formosa again. By the time she had paid a visit to Rembrandt's house and had a second trip around the canals, it was almost teatime. She strolled up the Kalverstraat once more, enjoying the shops. It was quite by chance that she came upon the small church, tucked away between two doorways; its own door stood open, and Maggy went in. It wasn't until she was inside that she realised that it was that enemy of her Calvinist forebears—a Popish church—but it was old and tranquil; she didn't think that the dominie at home would mind her being there.

She wandered around, looking at the windows and plaques, and then sat quietly, soothed by its peace and quiet, and thinking about England. She imagined herself back on the ward again, and was even able to convince herself that she would enjoy working hard

once more. She would write to Matron when she got
back to the Rapenburg, and within a week she would
be back at St Ethelburga's, her visit to Holland a fast-
fading dream. She stared at the beautiful altar through
tears, fiercely wiped away. 'Fool,' she whispered,
'greeting like a bairn; ye need yer tea, lass.' She
caught the gentle eye of Mary, poised beside her in
her niche. 'I shouldn't be here, but there's no harm
in telling ye.' She studied the calm sweet face. 'I
should have liked fine to be his wife and raised his
bairns.' She blew her nose, powdered it and smiled
at the little statue. And Mary smiled back, or so it
seemed, so that Maggy left the church quite com-
forted.

She had tea in the Bijenkorf—it was crowded and
noisy and gave her no chance to think; she felt better
after it, and crossed the Damrak to skirt the Dam
Square and walk down Nieuwendijk with plenty of
time for her train.

She was surprised to find Madame Riveau waiting
for her; she hadn't really expected her to take the
trouble to meet her again. She looked just as frightened as before, but this time there was another look
in the beady black eyes which Maggy couldn't understand. She stopped, listening with half-
comprehending ears to the woman's torrent of words.

'I hoped you'd come, Sister. I haven't been well,
but I had to do the shopping today, and I hoped that
I should see you, so I waited, and now I feel faint.'
She put a hand to her head. Certainly her face was
white.

Maggy said with real sympathy, 'I'm sorry ye're not well. Why don't ye go home to rest? It was nice to see you again.' She moved away from her companion, who caught hold of her arm.

'Sister, don't go! I feel dreadful: I live close by—please help me to my home, it's but two minutes' walk.'

Maggy hesitated. Madame Riveau did indeed look ghastly; she had time enough if she walked quickly—she didn't want to go with the woman, but in common humanity she couldn't leave her. The woman leaned heavily on her arm as they turned down the little alley; there was barely room for two to walk abreast. At the end of it they crossed a dreary little square and turned into a cul-de-sac lined on one side by a row of hideous little houses, fallen into dreadful decay, and facing a windowless length of grimy brick shed. Maggy hadn't seen anything so unlike Holland since she had arrived there. Halfway along the row, Madame Riveau stopped at what was surely the most dilapidated house of them all. The door stood half open, but the dirty windows, shrouded by even dirtier curtains, were shut. She leaned with her full weight against Maggy and said in a faint whining voice,

'Please come inside for a moment and help me to chair—and if I could have a little water...'

Maggy looked around. There was no one about, and she couldn't leave Madame Riveau to fend for herself; she would have to go in. She pushed the door wide open, and with her companion clinging to one arm, went inside.

The little house was horrid inside; small and dark
and meanly furnished. It smelled of dirt and damp
washing and badly cooked meals, and, Maggy suspected, a lack of decent sanitation. Madame Riveau,
still clutching her arm, drew her into what appeared
to be the living room, and Maggy's nostrils flared at
the increasing strength of the smells. She gently dis-
engaged herself, sat the woman down on a chair and
turned to the disgraceful sink, where she found a cup.
She cleaned it as best she could, filled it with water
and gave Madame Riveau one or two sips. To
Maggy's kindly and professional eye, she looked really ill—she looked at her watch; if she left now she
would be able to catch her train. On the other hand,
it would be nothing short of callous to leave Madame
Riveau alone. She stared at the silent figure on the
chair, and then gazed with distaste around the room
and made up her mind. She would make Madame
Riveau comfortable and then go and telephone a doctor; by then either her husband or son might have
returned, and she need not leave her alone.

Bed seemed the best thing. Maggy rotated slowly,
looking for a staircase and failing to find one—the
narrow passage led only to a cluttered little room with
a sink and tap in one corner. It smelled of mice, and
Maggy retreated to the living room to investigate the
doors in its walls. The first one was a cupboard, but
the double doors beside the stove revealed a large
alcove with a bed built into it like a bunk—Maggy
had seen something very like it that morning in a
museum, only that one had been spotlessly clean, with

gaily painted walls and bedlinen to shame the whitest
snow... She pulled back the blankets with a tentative
hand and wrinkled her nose and looked over her
shoulder at Madame Riveau. 'Sheets?' she asked
without much hope, and obeyed the feeble nod towards an old chest pushed against the wall. There
were sheets inside, and pillowcases, even a nightgown
of sorts, all of a uniform dingy grey, but better than
nothing.

Maggy stripped and made up the bed, eased Madame Riveau out of her clothes and into the nightgown, and helped her into the comparative comfort
of the stuffy little alcove, then looked once more at
her watch. It had all taken much longer than she had
expected. She had not only missed her train, she had
missed the next one as well. As soon as one of the
men came home—and that must surely be soon—they
would have to telephone Leiden as well as the doctor.
It wasn't very likely that she would be missed, at
least, not for an hour or so.

She picked up the pile of discarded sheets, smiled
reassuringly at Madame Riveau and went to the
kitchen, where, being of a practical turn of mind, she
set about finding a kettle, filling it and setting it on
the gas ring to boil before setting out on a tour of
inspection. The cupboard held a variety of food, all
of it quite unsuitable for Madame Riveau's stomach.
However, there was a bottle of milk which looked
fresh. Maggy uttered a cry of triumph and looked
round for something to boil it in. The saucepan she
found, even after she had scoured it, fell far short of

her standards of cleanliness, but it would have to do. She warmed some milk and took a little of it back to the bed. Madame Riveau drank it with an eagerness which made Maggy wonder when she had last had any, and asked for more.

'No,' said Maggy, 'for I don't know what's wrong with you.' She leaned down and tucked her in with a swift gentleness. 'Go to sleep. I'll stay until someone comes home.'

She collected a pile of dirty cups and plates on the table and went back to the kitchen; she might as well wash up while she was waiting. There was an apron hanging behind the door. She put it on, thinking ruefully that her new dress no longer looked new... She left the clean crocks to drain and eyed the furniture. There was another kettle of water on the boil; it would be a pity to sit and do nothing while she was waiting. The back door opened on to a small yard, damp and dark and sour-smelling. Maggy dumped the meagre furniture into it and set to with a will. Half an hour later, a bit grubby and dishevelled, she stood back and gave a satisfied nod. The kitchen was by no means spotless, but at least she could look at it now without feeling sick. She washed her hands and went to look at Madame Riveau, who, secure in her cupboard, had fallen asleep. She looked no better, indeed, her face was as grey as the sheets, but her pulse was stronger. Maggy opened the front door quietly and looked up and down the alley. There was no one to be seen and nothing to be heard except the subdued hum of the city all around her. She knocked at the doors on either side of her with no result, and then, rather desperately, tried each door in the row. The last three were boarded up anyway, ready for demolition, and there didn't seem to be anyone in any of the other houses. She went back indoors and found Madame Riveau awake. She fixed Maggy with a lustreless eye and muttered, 'Don't go.'

'Of course I won't,' said Maggy cheerfully, and when the woman's eyes had closed again, looked at her watch. She would be very late getting back to Leiden; she wondered if they had noticed her absence yet, and if they would be annoyed. They had a right to be—she was after all, Mevrouw Doelsma's nurse. Dr Doelsma would probably be icily, politely disapproving; yet what else could she do? She decided not to think about it; needless worry wouldn't help. With a gentle stealth and an economy of movement unexpected in so large a young woman, she started to put the odds and ends of furniture outside the front door, to attack them presently with renewed energy and a great deal of hot soapy water. Satisfied at length, she left them to dry and went back inside and started on the buffet. She had almost finished when both men arrived together. They stood in the doorway, staring at her, suspicious and unfriendly.

'Why are you here?' Monsieur Riveau asked surlily.

Maggy decided that it would take too long to explain in her slow-thinking French. 'Your wife's ill. Will you fetch a doctor quickly?'

He stood, not heeding her at all, looking across the room at his wife.

Maggy gave an impatient snort. 'Go on,' she said, 'hurry!' and was surprised when he turned and started walking rapidly away. Before the younger man had a chance to speak she turned to him.

'Will you get me another bucket of hot water, please, and then take the table outside.'

He muttered something and scowled at her to send a shiver down her back, but did as he was bid, and after watching her from the doorway for a minute he went into the kitchen. Maggy hitched the apron more securely around her waist and set to work on the floor. It was almost finished when she heard footsteps. There must have been a doctor living close by, or perhaps there was a hospital nearby. She wrung out the cloth, and with it in her hand, and still on her knees, turned round to see who Monsieur Riveau had brought with him.

He was, of course, the last man she had expected to see. It was a pity that just the sight of him should take her breath so that her voice, when she found it, was unsteady. Nevertheless, she contrived to say in her usual practical way,

'I'm so glad to see you, though I can't think how you came to be here.'

She smiled with relief and a delight she had forgotten to conceal, then saw that he had no intention of smiling back. His face was full of a thunderous anger which he hadn't troubled to conceal. He stood in the doorway staring at her, so that she was all at once very aware of the deplorable apron and the wisps of hair which had come loose. She put up an instinctive hand to tidy them away, then caught sight of its grubbiness and put it quickly behind her back.

He said with icy silkiness, 'It is only too obvious that you can't think. In your zeal—to—er—spring-clean this deplorable house, you appear to have over-looked that fact that you had a train to catch—and a patient expecting you back round about six o'clock.' He looked at his watch. 'It is now almost half past seven.'

Maggy dropped the cloth still in her hand into the bucket beside her, and wiped her grimy hand on the grimy apron. Her heart was beating unpleasantly fast, but she kept her voice calm.

'I didn't overlook anything,' she said quietly. 'I met Madame Riveau and she was ill and asked me to help her home. I couldn't leave her, so I started to tidy up a little.' She stopped, flushing, while he looked at the bucket of filthy water with raised eye-brows and a half smile which seemed to make non-sense of her words. Maggy felt rage bubble within her, and said in a shaking voice,

'If you think that I was neglectful of your mother, then I am sorry, though I must point out to you that your opinion could have no effect upon my actions as a nurse when I'm needed.'

It was disconcerting when he laughed at this neat speech. He was being hateful! She fixed her eyes on a level with his chin and said, 'Perhaps you will be good enough to look at Madame Riveau.' She took

off the apron and tossed it on to the buffet, trying not
to see the spots of dirty water on the new dress. Paul
shouldered his way past her without a word and bent
his length to look at the ill woman, and she, forgetful
of their quarrelling, made haste to help him. He was
quick and gentle and when he spoke his voice was
calmly reassuringly, so that Madame Riveau answered his questions willingly. When he at length
straightened up, he turned at once to the door.

'I'm going to ring the hospital and get an ambulance. She'll probably perforate—so the quicker they
look at her the better.' He paused, and looked over
his shoulder. 'If you have finished your scrubbing by
the time I come back, I can give you a lift to Leiden.'

Maggy didn't answer. She would have to go back
with him, anyway; it would be quicker. She handed
the bucket to Monsieur Riveau with a request for
more water; she might as well finish the floor.

She was ready and waiting when she heard the ambulance arrive and stop at the top of the alley. She
had scrubbed her hands and arms clean and dried
them on the hem of her slip and had tidied her hair;
the dress would have to wait until she got back. Paul
came in with the ambulance men and she just had
time to shake her patient's hand before she was carried away on the stretcher.

Paul stood at the door while she was being stowed
away, talking to the Riveau men, and presently they
too got into the ambulance. Neither of them had spoken to Maggy; she hadn't expected them to, anyway,
and turned away to tidy the bed and lock the back

door and turn off the gas. Paul followed her into the little kitchen, and stood watching her hang the apron on the door.

'What about the front door key?' she asked.

'I have it—it goes under a stone in the guttering. Are you ready?' She turned, to find him staring at her. 'That's a pretty dress,' he said equably.

Maggy took a long shuddering breath. 'Are you being beastly?' she asked in a hollow voice. 'It's new and this is the first time I've worn it, and now it's filthy and not pretty at all.'

She turned her back. She thought that she would probably burst into tears at any moment; the desire to do so was overwhelming. So she clamped her nice white teeth together and swallowed down the sobs crowding into her throat. She was succeeding very nicely when he said mildly,

'I'm not being—what was it?—beastly. You must surely know that a potato sack would look—nice—on you.'

Maggy gave a noisy gulp; his voice had sounded gentle and kind.

'Now you've made me cry!' she wailed, and burst into tears after all. Paul turned her round to face him and she made no effort to resist him. 'In that case, have my shoulder to cry on,' he said soothingly. His arm clamped her close while she sniffed and sobbed. She could feel his hand stroking the awful bird's nest of her hair, and presently it calmed her.

'Why were you so angry?' she asked in a watery voice, muffled by the cloth of his jacket.

Paul caught her by the shoulders, so that he could look intently into her damp, blotchy face.

'Is that why you are crying?'

Something in his voice made her heart beat faster. She blinked her puffy lids and stared steadily back at him.

'I'm sorry I was silly—it was because my dress was spoilt.' It was, after all, partly true.

He went on looking at her, and she fidgeted uneasily until he said, 'Of course,' in a dry voice, and went on, 'Here, take my handkerchief.'

He took a hand from her shoulder to search for one, and then stood, still holding her firmly while she dried her tears.

'We were all rather worried when you didn't arrive home—you see, you are always so punctual—and anything might have happened to you. I came into Amsterdam in case you...' he paused, 'no matter. I remembered that you had said that you might see Madame Riveau again, and I felt sure, from what you had said, that you had met her in the Nieuwendijk, so I left the car near the station and walked down on the chance of seeing you. I found Monsieur Riveau instead—I imagine that he shared my doubtful pleasure in renewing our acquaintance.'

Maggy was folding the handkerchief into a neat, sodden square. She said in a small resolute voice, 'I'm sorry if I've caused a bother; I didn't mean to, you know.' She gave the handkerchief a final pat and looked gravely at Paul. 'But I should do the same again...'

He took the handkerchief from her and stowed it in a pocket.

'Yes, I know you would; and you would be quite right, Maggy.' He bent his head and kissed her on the mouth, then stood back and said with a little smile, 'You'd better do something to that hair before we go, or people will think I've been ill-treating you!'

Maggy was glad of something to do. The kiss hadn't meant anything—not for Paul; but it had to her. She turned away and got a comb from her bag, then went into the little front room and did the best she could with her hair. It annoyed her that her hands were shaking so that the pins kept falling out again. She powdered her nose and lipsticked her mouth and felt better. She didn't look too bad in the miserable light of the gas jet. She turned it out and went back to the kitchen and said in a matter-of-fact voice, 'I'm ready, Dr Doelsma.'

It was quite chilly outside, she shivered as she waited for Paul to put the key in its hiding place. He caught her by the arm and started to walk briskly through the dark little cul-de-sac and across the small square to the alley leading to the Nieuwendijk. It was still full of people, most of them walking with the air of those on pleasure bent. Paul took the crown of the narrow street, Maggy's arm still firmly tucked in his. They had only gone a little way when he stopped and pulled her round to face him, ignoring the frustrated, good-natured cyclists weaving around them.

'You're shivering.'

'It's my own fault,' said Maggy soberly. 'It wasn't

really warm enough to wear this dress, but I—I wanted to...' Her voice died away uncertainly; she had remembered why she had wanted to wear the dress in the first place. Well, Paul had seen her in it, and a fine sight she had looked!

Paul had let go of her and was taking off his jacket. The comforting warmth of it was already around her shoulders when she started to protest.

'Paul, no! You can't walk through Amsterdam in shirtsleeves and a waistcoat!'

'You called me Paul,' he said quietly.

Maggy felt her face getting hot, and was glad of the dark. 'I wasna' thinking—I didna' guard my tongue...will you take your jacket back?'

He caught her by the arm again, and started to walk her along at a great rate.

'Don't be silly,' was all he said.

Maggy was glad of her long legs to keep up with his. She peeped sideways at him and saw that he was frowning fiercely.

'I'm sorry if I've been tiresome.'

'I've already told you not to be silly.'

There seemed no point in continuing even so meagre a conversation as theirs was. Maggy held her tongue, and continued to do so, sitting quietly in the car beside Paul and saying, 'Yes, Dr Doelsma. No, Dr Doelsma' in appropriate context to the few remarks he made on their homeward journey. When they reached his house, she jumped out quickly, thankful to find the door open. Anny was hovering in the hall. She gave her Paul's jacket, and started up the stairs. She was out of sight by the time he appeared in the doorway.

Mevrouw Doelsma was in her room, lying comfortably on a chaise-longue. She put down her book when she saw Maggy and said in a relieved voice,

'Maggy, there you are! We have all been so worried about you. Fortunately Paul came home early and went at once to Amsterdam. Sit down and tell me all about it; dinner can wait.'

It was during that meal, half an hour later, that it was decided that they should return the following day to Oudehof. Maggy sat listening to the discussion. She wouldn't see much more of Paul—she would be returning to England very soon now; probably before he paid another visit to his mother. She sighed at the sadness of her thoughts, and Paul said,

'Will you be sorry to leave Leiden, Maggy?'

She assumed a determinedly cheerful face. 'Yes, Doctor, but Oudehof is lovely too.'

He nodded. 'A pity you won't be here for the skating.'

It was a nice safe topic, and lasted them until the meal was finished and she was able to slip upstairs and leave Mevrouw Doelsma and Paul to their nightly game. When she went down later to suggest that her patient went to bed, he gave her a cursory glance, wished her goodnight and remarked in casual tones that he would see her in the morning. She waited until she had shepherded Mevrouw Doelsma to the door before replying in a colourless voice,

'Very well, Dr Doelsma—and thank you for bringing me back this evening, and for being so…so…'

He stood looking at her, his mouth faintly curved in a smile.

'Magnanimous?' he suggested.

There were sparks in Maggy's eyes; she drew a deep breath.

'Whatever you say, Doctor,' she said. It was amusing to him, she supposed, to tease her. She started to shut the door.

'You haven't said goodnight, Maggy.'

She paused and looked over her shoulder. 'Goodnight, Doctor.'

'Paul,' he interrupted. He was smiling, and her heart gave a lurch.

'Goodnight, Paul,' she said obediently, and shut the door.

There was no sign of Paul when she went down to breakfast the following morning—Anny offered the information that the doctor had gone out early and would be back later. Maggy ate without appetite and went upstairs to get Mevrouw Doelsma ready for her journey. It was ten o'clock before they were ready and made their way down to the hall. Dr Doelsma was sitting on one of the carved chairs ranged against the wall, reading a newspaper. He looked up unhurriedly as they approached and got up, bidding them a cheerful good morning. His mother turned to make her farewells to Anny, and Maggy found herself a little apart, under a leisurely scrutiny from Paul. She drew her brows together and looked haughtily away, the hateful colour, creeping up her cheeks. She had dressed with care in a blue-green tweed suit, its velvet collar exactly matching the beret which went with it. Her shoes and handbag weren't new, but they were good and beautifully polished. With female logic she had wanted to look her best for this, their probable last meeting. Even if he saw her again, she would most likely be in uniform.

It was a pity that her gaze had settled on a portrait of a Doelsma ancestor—it might have been Paul gazing down at her from the canvas, with the same dark eyebrows and smile.

Paul said softly in her ear, 'Poor Maggy, we're all round you, aren't we?'

She had lost her breath and made do with a dignified nod, only to be plunged into further confusion by his remarking,

'You look delightful. Without retracting anything I may have said about potato sacks, I must admit that your obvious charms are greatly enhanced. Why have I not seen it before? It seems to me that whenever we have met you have been entrenched behind your uniform—you look delightful in that too, but intimidating.'

Maggy raised astonished eyes to his. She asked uncertainly, 'Me? Intimidating?'

'Oh, yes. I was quite terrified of you at St Ethelburga's when we went round your ward.' He went on gravely, his eyes twinkling, 'As stiff as a poker—I longed to pinch you to see if you were real. I kissed you instead, if you remember.' Maggy blushed, and he stood and watched her. 'It was a great relief to find that you were.'

Maggy cast around for an answer to this and failed to find one; it was fortunate that Mevrouw Doelsma was on the point of rejoining them, she would get her goodbyes said quickly. She raised her lovely eyes to Paul and opened her mouth and was on the point of uttering when he said, reading her thoughts, 'My dear good girl, don't say goodbye. I'm driving you back to Oudehof.' He grinned and took his mother's arm, leaving her to take her leave of Anny. When she got outside, Mevrouw Doelsma was already sitting in the back of the car, and Paul was waiting by the open door. 'Get in front,' he said, in a voice which brooked no argument.

Maggy got in without a word and sat passive while he fastened her seat-belt. Her thanks, uttered in a meek voice, caused him to look at her with suspicion.

'You're remarkably humble,' he remarked. She ignored both the tone and the look, and instead looked over her shoulder to where his mother was sitting in the back of the car.

'Mevrouw Doelsma, would you not prefer me to sit with you?'

Her patient barely glanced up from the pile of letters in her lap.

'No, dear. You see I have all these letters to read, and a shopping list to make out for Mrs Pratt—such a good idea of Paul's that I should save myself the trouble of doing it once we get back to Oudehof.' She opened an envelope, smiled vaguely in Maggy's direction, and became at once immersed in its contents.

Paul started the car. 'Never mind,' he said in a maddeningly sympathetic voice, 'It's only for a couple of hours.'

Maggy caught his smile and found herself smiling back and decided, with her usual good sense, to enjoy the present. The future, bleak though it was going to be, could take care of itself, so she sat back composedly, giving no sign of her thumping heart, and was glad when Paul did not appear to notice her pink cheeks and breathless voice.

Once out of Leyden and on to the broad motorway, he started a gentle flow of inconsequential talk which put her so much at her ease that she forgot to be shy, and was soon chattering away with an enjoyment which she refrained from reminding herself would be but short-lived. After fifteen minutes or so, Paul turned off the Amsterdam road. 'We'll go through Haarlem,' he said, 'and Alkmaar. You might as well see as much of Holland as you can before you go back.'

Maggy turned her head to look out of the window; she hadn't wanted to be reminded. She said in a carefully cheerful voice. 'How kind of you. I shall have such a lot to remember...'

She watched the green meadows bordering the road—each with its complement of cows, neatly coated against the chill of autumn. 'I mustn't remember,' she thought. 'I must forget as quickly as possible—perhaps if I'm very busy.' She became aware that he had spoken. 'I'm sorry,' she said. 'I was thinking.'

He smiled slowly; she couldn't see his eyes beneath their drooping lids.

'Madame Riveau asked me to thank you for your help yesterday.' He gentled the Rolls to a smooth standstill, while the road ahead of them lifted itself on a giant hinge to allow a barge of incredible length to ooze its way beneath it on the canal bisecting the road.

Maggy felt contrite. 'Madame Riveau! How awful of me to forget her. Did you telephone the hospital—is she all right?'

The bridge started to swing down. Paul, with his eyes on the traffic lights, said, 'I went to see her this morning—they operated last night. She should do well now—no thanks to those graceless menfolk of hers.'

The Rolls surged ahead again. Maggy took a quick look behind her, to see Mevrouw Doelsma still happily reading her letters. 'I'm glad she'll be well again—she worried me when I had her on my ward at St Ethelburga's.'

'You take your work very seriously, don't you?' Paul asked.

Maggy raised her eyes to his. 'Don't you, too, Doctor?'

His eyes were on the road ahead. They were approaching Haarlem, and he slowed down. 'I? Of course, but I have the advantage over you, have I not?

For when I marry, I shall have a wife and children to fill my life, as well as my work.'

The pain in her heart seemed physical. 'You mean that I have only my job? But that keeps me very busy.'

'Don't you want to marry, Maggy?' he asked casually.

'I'm quite happy, Doctor,' she said, and gasped as he said,

'You're a poor liar, my girl,' and before she could think of a reply, 'Mama, shall we stop in Alkmaar for coffee and show Maggy the cheese market?'

The conversation became three-cornered and stayed so until they entered Alkmaar, when Paul slowed the car so that Maggy might admire the grass-encircled water before they entered its narrow streets. It was getting on for midday, and the streets were pleasantly bustling.

'What a cosy place!' Maggy cried.

Paul agreed. 'Though it wasn't always so—the Spaniards laid siege to it in the sixteenth century, you know. I imagine it was far from cosy then.'

They had reached the end of the main street, and he turned the car into a very narrow street, lined with small shops. It opened rather unexpectedly on to a cobbled area, with a canal on one side and a row of houses and shops on the other. In its centre stood the Weigh-House, its delightful step gables climbing upwards, to culminate in a weather vane. Paul parked the Rolls just beyond this fairy-tale edifice and looked at his watch.

'We're just in time to see the clock. Jump out, Maggy.' He leaned across her and undid her belt and opened the door. 'We'll be back in a moment, Mama.'

Maggy found herself being hustled over the cobbles, just in time to watch the quaint little figures appear as the clock chimed. She stood gazing upwards, her eyes alight with interest, her lovely mouth slightly open. Paul stood beside her, an arm flung carelessly around her shoulders. When it was finished she said, 'I think the bells and chimes are the things I'll remember most. They're so beautiful.'

They started back towards the car, walking slowly, his arm still around her while he told her of the town. They collected Mevrouw Doelsma and crossed the cobbles to a small unpretentious café facing them. It was warm and very clean and smelled appetisingly of soup with a distinct whiff of brandy. They sat at a table covered with what Maggy thought was a run, and drank delicious coffee, while the proprietor stood chatting to them. She had to admire the way Paul contrived to translate for her, without interrupting the flow of the conversation.

The weather had clouded over by the time they left the café. There was a cold wind blowing; it ruffled the canal water and made the trees rustle dryly. They got back into the car and Paul drove out of the little town on to the Den Helder road; it ran alongside a canal, running as straight as a ruler through the flat bare country. Maggy didn't care for it, and said so. Paul agreed. 'But I came this way so that you could

see as much of Holland as possible. It isn't all as
beautiful as the country around Oudehof.'

The road was empty ahead of them. The Rolls
flashed along without hindrance. The tall blocks of
flats on the outskirts of Den Helder appeared on the
skyline. Maggy looked at them with a critical eye and
offered the opinion that it appeared to be an ugly
place.

'Very ugly,' said Mevrouw Doelsma. 'Fortunately
you aren't likely to come this way again; I shall close
my eyes,' she added, 'and you can tell me when we
get to Hippolytushoef, for there it is much prettier.'

This she did, leaving Paul to point out the meagre
attractions of the town and then to explain the far
more interesting details of the dyke they were about
to cross. They went sedately through the great sluices
and on to the road under the great sea dyke wall.
Maggy thought it was a pity that it hid the sea from
their sight, but the Ijlselmeer on their other side held
sufficient of interest to keep her busy asking questions
for the first few miles. Paul answered her carefully
and with no sign of impatience, until she paused and
asked, 'Am I boring you? It must be tedious for you
to tell me all this...'

They were approaching the café half way along the
Afsluitdijk. The car leapt ahead, eating up distance
with effortless ease, as the needle crept up and up.
Paul looked at her, and said, unsmiling,

'You never bore me, Maggy, and never will. I
thought you knew that.'

'No. I didn't know,' said Maggy. Happiness

swelled up inside her; it wouldn't last, but it would be something to treasure—something she wouldn't forget. She fidgeted like an awkward child, knowing that he was looking at her.

'All right, you want to change the subject, don't you?' He scarcely waited for her nod. 'That's Friesland ahead—once we're on the mainland, we turn off for Bolsward.'

She watched the coastline rushing to meet them, grey against a grey sky, and presently they passed through a tongue of land, standing forlornly with a single row of small houses and a tiny lock, abandoned by the mainland. There was a woman hanging washing on a line in one of the back gardens, and no one else to be seen.

'Do people really live there?' Maggy wanted to know, 'What do they do?'

'Work on the *dijk,* fish...' Paul answered carelessly. 'It's called Kornwerderzand.'

They laughed at her attempts to pronounce it, but after half a dozen attempts she thought she did it rather well—it was another word to add to her small vocabulary.

The mainland was reached and with it the Friesian farmsteads, standing solidly, backed by their enormous barns and surrounded by their acres of rolling meadows. Mevrouw Doelsma gave a satisfied sigh.

'Oh, how nice to be back! I love Leiden, but this is my home.'

'Mother's a dyed-in-the-wool Friesian in everything but size,' Paul teased gently. 'Fortunately for her self-esteem, the girls and I managed to achieve the height and size she had set her heart on.'

He had pulled into the side of the road while a high, wide farm cart, drawn by a magnificent Flemish horse, rolled slowly past.

'Yes, I have been so glad about that,' murmured his mother, 'and now all the children are shooting up so satisfactorily,' she sighed. 'I hope yours will be true Friesians, Paul.'

They were moving again, and on the outskirts of Bolsward.

'We shall have to wait and see, shan't we, Mother?' Paul answered blandly, and then, 'Look on your left, Maggy, here's the Gemeentehuis you so much admired.'

She looked obediently, glad to have her thoughts diverted, and asked intelligent questions which kept the conversation safely impersonal, if slightly dull. It was a relief to leave Sneek behind and know that the journey was almost over. Probably Paul would go straight back after a late lunch. She fell silent, weighed down by the possibility that she would probably not see him again and that there was nothing that she could do about it. It was with feelings of relief that she saw that they were approaching Oudehof. They swept through the gates, and as Paul stopped the car, the front door opened to reveal Pratt, who had gone back several days earlier, his elderly sombre face wreathed in rare smiles. Mrs Pratt came bustling across the hall as they went in and in a surprisingly short time had them sitting down to the excellent luncheon she had prepared for them.

They had eaten their smoked filleted eel on its hot buttered toast, and were half way through the *Rolpens met Rodekool*—spiced and pickled minced beef and tripe and apples and red cabbage—when Mevrouw Doelsma, who had been talking about nothing in particular, asked,

'Paul, do you have to go back at once?'

He put down his knife and fork and sat back in his high-backed chair so that he could watch Maggy.

'No, Mama. If I may, I'll stay until tomorrow morning.'

Maggy's hands tightened on her own knife and fork, but she didn't look up when his mother said,

'Of course you may stay, Paul. What nonsense to ask when it's your house! I felt sure you would want to go to Utrecht.' He made no answer and she went on airily, 'I suppose I shall have to rest until teatime. May I not lie down on the sofa in the drawing room—just for once?' She looked enquiringly at Maggy, who smiled and said comfortably that she didn't see why not—just for once, and then relapsed into silence while Paul and his mother discussed the visits she was planning to make to her daughters.

It was as they were leaving the dining room that Mevrouw Doelsma said,

'Why don't you take Maggy for a walk, Paul? I'm sure you would both enjoy the exercise.'

Maggy watched the dark brows gather in a frown before he answered shortly. His, 'Yes, of course,' was uninviting. 'Would you like that, Maggy?' He barely glanced at her.

Maggy gave him a cool stare. She loved him with her whole heart, but he could annoy her very much too! 'I think not, thank you, Dr Doelsma, there are several things I should like to do before tea.'

She might have saved her breath. As he opened the door for them to pass through, he said coolly,

'I have some telephone calls to make. I'll be in the study…about ten minutes, if that suits you?'

She made no answer; what was the use? She wasn't going to stand there wrangling about a walk, but she had no intention of going with him, not after that frown. Besides, she told herself for the hundredth time, the less she saw of him before she went back to England, the better.

She followed Mevrouw Doelsma into the drawing room and unhurriedly set about making her comfortable on the large velvet-covered sofa before the log fire, and lingered about her small tasks in the beautiful room, until, lying back against high-piled cushions, glasses and book within reach, her patient said, 'There, Maggy, there's not another thing I want. Go and enjoy your walk.'

But Maggy lingered. 'Would you not like me to read to you, Mevrouw Doelsma?'

'Not today, my dear. I shall go to sleep at once.'

She closed her eyes in proof of her statement, and Maggy walked reluctantly to the door. It was a large double one, but it opened noiselessly under her hand; she closed it quietly behind her. The walls of the old house were very thick, but she didn't think anyone—Paul—would hear her. The study door was across the hall to her left, and she kept her eyes on it as she took off her shoes. If she could get upstairs to her room he would probably forget about the wretched walk. There was a vast expanse of black and white tiles between her and the staircase. Maggy started to cross it, her eyes on the door.

She had almost reached the stairs when she froze at Paul's voice. Without turning round she knew where he was. There was a great chair by one of the console tables on the right of the drawing room door...she hadn't even glanced that way.

'Were you thinking of changing your shoes? There's no need, you know. It isn't wet underfoot.' He was gently mocking; she knew that if she looked at him, he would be smiling. She sat down deliberately on the bottom stair and put on her shoes.

'I did say that I would prefer not to go for a walk, Doctor,' she said in a reasonable voice. 'I meant it.' She ventured to look at him. Yes, he was smiling—she looked away quickly, and reiterated, 'There are some things I wish to do.'

He had got up from his chair. 'Something very secret,' he remarked affably, 'since it requires you to creep about the house in your stockings.' He walked over to where she was standing on the lowest stair, and despite her own six feet, he still looked down at her. 'And now tell me the real reason. Maggy.'

She said, very calm and composed. 'You frowned...you looked quite—quite saturnine. I have no intention of going for a walk with someone who finds the prospect so unwelcome.'

She turned on her heel and started up the stairs, to be caught round the waist and swung round and put gently on her feet beside him.

He released her at once. 'Maggy, I'm sorry. What an ill-mannered boor you must think me.' His grey eyes looked very bright; she wanted to look away and found she couldn't. 'Will it be enough if I say that I should very much like to go walking with you?'

It was impossible to say no when he was looking at her like that. She went over to the table where she had put hat and gloves, and he followed her over and opened a drawer, pulled out a scarf and tossed it to her.

'Here,' he said lightly, 'tie your hair up in this— there's a wind blowing.'

They went out of the door together and started down the short drive.

'Let's go to the village—have you seen the church?'

'No,' said Maggy. 'It's always shut, and I didn't know how to ask for the key.'

He gave her a brief look. 'Poor girl, we've treated you very badly. You've been left a great deal to your own devices, haven't you?'

Maggy looked surprised. 'I'm not on holiday, Doctor.'

Paul looked as though he was about to say something else, but he remained silent, striding along the pleasant road. Maggy for once was glad to match him for size; anyone smaller would have been running by now... Stien, for instance. She squashed the thought—she would enjoy herself; had Paul not said that he had wanted to take her walking? She looked at him and met the same bright gaze she had found so disturbing in the hall. He blinked rapidly and his eyes were their usual cool grey once more.

'We're on a dead dyke,' he explained. Maggy stood still and looked around her. They were indeed walking above the level of the fields all around them. But the sea was several miles away.

'It's not needed any more,' she hazarded. 'You reclaimed the land, and so another dyke was built...'

'Clever girl!' He sounded pleased at her interest. By the time they reached the village, he had told her all about Sleepers and Dreamers and Watchers.

'Such lovely names,' she said. 'They sound like sentinels on duty.'

Paul smiled. 'But that's just what they are,' he said.

They were in the village by now and he slowed his pace a little. The few people about greeted him with smiles and nods and incomprehensible words.

'We like to speak our own language,' he explained briefly as he knocked on the door of a very small house indeed; the end one in a similar row. 'You were disgusted with Madame Riveau's house, weren't you? Now you shall see how a Friesian housewife keeps house.'

The woman who answered the door was big and tall—as tall as Maggy herself—but no longer young.

When she saw Paul she beamed and shook hands, and when he introduced Maggy, wrung her hand too.

'We're to go inside and have tea—Mevrouw Stijlma is the sexton's wife; we can get the keys of the church from her.'

The three of them almost filled the tiny room. Maggy, pushed gently into a chair by Paul, looked around her with interest.

'May I stare?' she enquired of him. 'I know it's rude, but there's so much to see.'

The room sparkled and shone with a perfection of cleanliness Maggy had seldom seen. The walls were almost covered with enlarged photos, some of them a dingy brown with age, and all framed in dark wood. They jostled some of the most beautiful plates; worthy of a museum. The mantelpiece was shrouded in plum-coloured chenille with an important bobble fringe; it held brass candlesticks of as fine a workmanship as could be found. She guessed that they were probably two hundred years old. The furniture was solid and Victorian in style and draped in snowy antimacassars, but the wooden chairs round the table were painted in the traditional bright colours of Hindeloopen and were a great deal older than the rest of the furniture.

Paul left her to gaze her fill, and then asked, 'Well?'

'It's so clean. I mean everything—and some of the things are beautiful.'

Her startled eye lighted on a large woollen square hung on the wall, woven into a startling picture of unlikely kittens and a ball of very pink wool. Next to it hung a sampler, exquisitely stitched and almost colourless with age.

'Things get handed down from one generation to another.' Paul's eyes were twinkling. 'There's quite a variety.'

They drank their tea, milkless and in paper-thin cups, while he and the sexton's wife talked with little pauses while the conversation was translated for Maggy's benefit. After a little while they took their leave, the church keys swinging from Paul's hand.

It was a large church, old and rather austere, with a thin spire crowned by its weathercock. Paul opened the low wide door and it creaked ajar to let them pass through. It was quiet and cool inside, with plain white-washed walls and no stained glass windows or ornaments, and no flowers. Maggy found it very much to her taste, for it reminded her of the bare little church near her own home. It seemed natural for Paul to take her hand and lead her down the centre aisle between the high wooden pews with their carved ends, each with its card, neatly inserted in its brass holder, bearing the names of its occupants. He stopped by the front pew and she stooped down to see his name, Van Beijen Doelsma, and his mother's name beneath it, and when she looked at the stone flags they were standing upon, his name was there too. The letters were impossible to understand but the name was clear and the date: 1649.

She said quietly, 'It makes you feel small, doesn't it?' and then, 'You really belong here, don't you?'

They were peering up at a wall plaque, a riot of carved plumes, elaborate scrolls and cherubim arranged around the stone profile of a haughty-looking gentleman with a determined chin and a Napoleonic hairstyle.

'Great-great-Grandfather,' said Paul. 'He didn't take kindly to being occupied by the French troops under Napoleon. He spent a lot of time in prison, leaving his wife to bring up six children—they're all here—each generation follows the same pattern of life as the previous one. We are christened and married and buried here.' He looked down at her. 'And I shall follow that pattern.'

Maggy had a sudden blindingly vivid picture of Stien standing in the aged church, a vision in white satin and tulle. She said hastily, to forget it, 'Won't that be rather difficult for you? You work in Leiden and you are often in Utrecht.'

They moved slowly side by side down the aisle and contemplated the magnificent sounding-board above the pulpit.

'I shan't need to go to Utrecht so often,'—Maggy silently agreed; he would have Stien with him always, wouldn't he?—'We'll spend the week in Leiden and come up here for weekends, and my wife and children will do the same.'

'Naturally,' murmured Maggy. She supposed Stien wouldn't mind—after all, she would have the best of both worlds and Paul for a husband; what more could any girl want?

They wandered slowly to the door and so out into

the late afternoon and back down the road to return
the keys to Mevrouw Stijlma, and when they turned
to leave, Maggy, rather shyly, said, '*Dag,* Mevrouw,'
which released a flood of kindly praise, not one word
of which she could understand.

'Very nice,' said Paul. 'Have you managed to ac-
quire any Dutch while you've been in Holland?' He
sounded really interested, and Maggy was emboldened to recite her vocabulary—a hotch-potch of
words she had heard and remembered to look up in
her dictionary. He laughed a good deal at some of
them, and spent the whole of the walk back to Oudehof explaining the complications of Dutch grammar
to her. Maggy listened attentively and thought wistfully that there were more interesting things to talk of
other than the pitfalls to be found in the Dutch language.

The afternoon had become unpleasantly chilly by
the time they had reached the house. Great clouds
billowed over the wide sky, the wind tore at Maggy's
headscarf and whipped her hair around her face. The
hall was warm and welcoming. Maggy stood at the
foot of the staircase, taking off her gloves. Her face
glowed with the chill; her eyes sparkled. She refused
Paul's offer of tea and in reply to his enquiry as to
whether she had enjoyed her walk, said soberly,

'Aye, it was a grand wee walk, Dr Doelsma. Thank
you for showing me the kirk...'

He interrupted her rather impatiently.

'There's no question of thanks, Maggy. I don't
know when I have enjoyed a walk so much, perhaps

because I seldom have the chance of airing my knowledge to such a good listener as yourself.'

'Och, aye,' Maggy said shortly. Her brows knitted into a frown; she was suddenly out of temper with her world. If it had been Stien with Paul, it wouldn't have mattered what sort of a listener he had…

'I'm away to Mevrouw Doelsma.' She didn't look at him, but went upstairs at a great rate, her long legs taking two steps at a time.

By the time she had left Mevrouw Doelsma there wasn't more than half an hour to dinner. She changed rapidly into the pink dress and pinned her hair neatly. It was still damp from her bath and she brushed the curly tendrils tidily aside, and then, when they sprang loose again, threw down her brush with an unwonted impatience, and with barely a second glance in the mirror went down to the drawing room to find Mevrouw Doelsma and the doctor already there.

Dinner passed pleasantly enough. The talk was of the kind that needed very little thought, the food and pleasant surroundings had their effect on her. Maggy rose from the table quite cheerful and went as usual to her room while Paul and his mother had their hour or so together. It was almost ten o'clock when she returned to the drawing room. Mevrouw Doelsma was more than ready for bed and got up at once and kissed her son. 'Goodnight, Paul. I'll see you before you go in the morning.'

'Of course.' He looked at Maggy standing quietly near the door. She said goodnight, too, but he didn't answer at once, and she turned to go. He said, at his most persuasive, 'Come riding in the morning, Maggy? Is seven o'clock too early for you?'

She hadn't meant to say yes. She was half way up the stairs, still trying to decide why she had been so weak-willed, and at the same time bubbling over with happiness.

It was a wild grey morning, but dry, Maggy was at the stables well before the hour, to find the doctor gentling Cobber and Biddy ready for her. They swung into the saddles and started off across the park and out into the little lane at its back, not hurrying, but talking idly. She was completely taken by surprise when Paul said casually,

'I should like to take you out, Maggy. Perhaps we could have dinner and dance somewhere, if you would like that.'

She took so long to reply that he turned to look at her.

'Of course, if you don't want to, my dear girl, don't hesitate to say so.'

'Of course I want to come!' Maggy burst out, and stopped. She did, but was it rather unwise? She squashed her more prudent thoughts, and said, 'You see, I haven't a dress.'

He chuckled. 'That's the first time I've heard that used as an excuse for not going on a date! Usually it's the other way round; surely an invitation is a good reason for buying a new dress?'

They turned the horses and started for home.

'Mother shall go with you to Leeuwarden. You

may have discovered already that she loves to shop. There's bound to be something to fit you there. They cater for big women here, you know.'

Maggy said indignantly, 'I wish you wouldn't call me a big woman!'

He gave her a sideways glance; there was a gleam in his eye. 'Certainly I won't call you a big woman if you don't like it. I can think of several alternatives—shall I try out a few?'

Maggy frowned. 'No,' she said severely.

He said. 'Just as you like, Maggy,' in a deceptively meek voice, so that she had to laugh. 'That's better,' he said. 'Now about this evening…'

He left soon after breakfast, and his mother came down to see him off.

'You'll be in Leiden for lunch,' she remarked.

'I'm going to Utrecht, Mother.' He was stuffing papers into a briefcase.

'I can't think why you don't live there!' his mother declared rather pettishly.

'Yes, you can, dearest. You know how much I am attached to my home in Leiden, I could never give it up. Besides, my son must inherit it in his turn, must he not?'

Maggy, standing rather uncertainly close by, not sure if she was wanted, heard him. He looked very handsome and more arrogant than ever. She thought of him in his house on the Rapenburg, with a very large family and a devoted and well-loved wife. She couldn't bear it and turned to slip quietly upstairs, but he had seen her move and put out a long arm and swung her round to walk with them to the door, where he kissed his mother, then turned and dropped a light kiss on the tip of her own nose and got into his car and drove away.

He had said that he was coming back in two days' time to take her out. Maggy had plenty of time to think about it meanwhile. She supposed that the evening out was a kind of thank-you from a grateful employer. She would be going back to England in a few days, just as soon as she heard from Matron. Paul, she thought without conceit, had grown to like her as a friend, and there was no reason why two friends shouldn't have a pleasant evening together. She hadn't expected to see him again; she would make the most of what would most certainly be their last meeting.

CHAPTER EIGHT

MAGGY STOOD in front of the mirror in her bedroom at Grotehof, and looked at herself. She supposed she was all right—it was a pity that there was so much of her—but the dress was certainly rather nice, cream guipure lace over a matching slip with a narrow blue velvet ribbon at the waist. It just skimmed her knees, showing off her long legs to advantage; it was sleeveless too. She had been rather doubtful about so much bosom showing, but Mevrouw Doelsma had told her that a low décolleté was quite a proper thing.

Maggy gave her hair a final pat, picked up her little evening purse and went downstairs. Paul and his mother were sitting by the fire in the hall. He saw her first and got up and came towards her, looking elegant and immensely tall. She stood shyly on the bottom step while he looked her frankly up and down.

'Delightful, Maggy. I can see that you will turn all the men's heads this evening.'

But not yours, Paul, she thought, and added out loud, 'Och, who'd want to look at a great lass like me?'

She went over to the fire to show herself to Mevrouw Doelsma, who pronounced herself more than satisfied with Maggy's appearance.

'I'll get my coat,' said Maggy, but before she could take more than a couple of steps, Paul stopped her.

'It will be quite chilly later on—it's a long drive.' He took no notice of her look of surprise, but went on, 'I wondered if you would like to borrow Cousin Marthe's coat—it's only gathering dust in a closet upstairs.' He lifted an armful of superb cashmere coat from the back of one of the chairs, and stood holding it out.

Maggy put out a hand and touched it. 'It's beautiful!' she breathed. 'It looks like cashmere.'

'It is cashmere,' he answered.

'But I can't wear it; what would your cousin say?'

The doctor looked at her, his head a little on one side.

'Nothing at all,' he said, with perfect truth. He strode forward and wrapped it around Maggy. 'It fits you very well, too,' he said, avoiding his mother's eye.

Maggy walked slowly over to the large gilt-framed mirror on one wall, and stood in front of it, stroking the coat gently. 'I've never had a cashmere coat,' she murmured. She looked anxiously at the doctor over one shoulder. 'Is it not impertinent to wear something so costly? I mean—' she sought for words—'I would never be able to buy a coat like this one in my whole life.'

Paul was getting into his own coat and replied easily,

'Well, if it were an old coat, you'd not think twice about it, would you? But we haven't an old tweed

coat to fit you, so you'll have to do with this one.'
He didn't give Maggy time to think too deeply about
this, but he had spoken in such a matter-of-fact voice
that her face cleared and she walked over to Mevrouw
Doelsma with her doubt dispelled, and said goodnight
before going out to the car with the doctor.

It was barely half-past six. Paul allowed the Rolls
to idle along the narrow road to Heerenveen, but once
on the main road to the south he allowed the needle
to creep up to the hundred mark and steady itself
there. He settled himself so that he could watch her
face, and said,

'Do you like travelling fast, Maggy?'

'Aye, I like it fine, Doctor.' She gave him a fleeting
smile. 'Though I'd not dare myself,' she added truth-
fully. 'I'd not feel safe.'

'I trust you feel safe with me?'

She laughed. 'You know I do, Doctor.'

He sighed loudly. 'Maggy, must we have this for-
mality? If my memory serves me aright, you've called
me Paul on previous occasions.'

She said, with rather a heightened colour, 'Well, I
was a wee bit fashed...'

'Is it only when you're fashed that you forget to
guard your tongue, Maggy?'

She made a fierce little sound; the weak ghostling
of some old Gaelic word. 'I shall not say, Doc...'

'Paul,' he said.

'Paul,' she finished.

He chuckled and gentled the Rolls back to a la-
dylike pace as they went through Amersfoort, so that

he could point out some of the more interesting aspects of the pleasant town. 'We're almost there,' he said.

Maggy gave him a questioning look. 'It's a long way to come for dinner,' she said. 'Wasn't there anything nearer Oudehof?'

The doctor's lips twitched as he thought of the numbers of young ladies who had been only too glad to travel for an hour in his company.

'Is my company so irksome?' he asked. 'I thought you would like the ride; I'm sorry if you have found it boring.'

He kept his attention on the road as they passed an articulated lorry, travelling hell-for-leather from Germany to the coast; he was trying not to laugh.

Maggy gave a gasp, and put a hand on his knee, 'I didn't mean that,' she uttered. 'You must know I didn't, I wanted to go out with you.' She took a sharp breath—she hadn't meant to say quite that—and made haste to modify it. 'I mean,' she said carefully, 'you've gone to so much trouble to arrange the evening, even finding a coat for me—and there must be any number of hotels near Leeuwarden where we could have gone, and you need not have spent the entire evening…' She stopped. He had steered the car into the slow traffic lane, and now he took a hand off the wheel and covered hers with it. He wasn't laughing any more.

'Maggy, stop! Why do you suppose I asked you out this evening?'

'Well, Doc… Paul,' she explained, 'I think it's

a…a kind of treat because my job is finished and I'll be leaving…'

'A sweet after the medicine?' he asked quietly.

'Aye, that's it.'

He pulled into the side of the motorway and stopped the car, then turned deliberately in his seat so that he could see her.

'I asked you out because I wanted to spend an evening with you, Maggy—I enjoy your company. I am not giving you a treat—I am the one who is having that. You could have easily refused to come.'

She looked back at him steadily. 'I never thought to do that,' she replied honestly.

He switched on the engine again. 'Having cleared up that knotty little problem, let's dine. I hope you're hungry, for I'm famished. Years ago, I took a girl out to dinner at this same place. She was very small and dainty and had an appetite to match. She refused almost all solid food, and I spent a dreadful evening, dancing on an empty stomach.' They laughed together and fell into a comfortable discussion about food, until he drew up outside the imposing doors of the Hotel Kasteel Hooge Vuursche. Maggy found its splendid magnificence rather overpowering, but she suffered the cashmere coat to be taken from her, and followed the waiter to a table on the edge of the dance floor. Paul following her, nodded to several acquaintances, and watched the interested glances cast at Maggy. She didn't seem to notice them, but sat down with charming dignity, as though she were in the habit of dining there every evening. She studied the menu card, and

Paul picked up his own and waited, not sure if her schoolgirl French could cope with it. Presently he said, 'Is there anything particular you would like, or will you leave it to me?'

She gave him a grateful glance. 'Please will you choose? Though I would very much like to try the *caneton à la Rouennaise*'—she pronounced it beautifully.

The doctor wondered where she had got her knowledge of the famous dish, but was far too well-mannered to ask; but she seemed to think that an explanation was due to him.

'I've never eaten it—I've never been to a restaurant grand enough to serve it—but the laird—my father is his factor—used to walk with me sometimes and talk about food, and it was one of the dishes he told me I must try if ever I had the opportunity.'

'It's an excellent choice, Maggy. Shall we have *consommé* first and then *Sole Normande*, and finish with a *bombe bouché aux fruits?*'

'It sounds lovely.' She looked around her while he conferred with the waiter. This done, he sat back in his chair and said,

'And now I'll answer the questions I can see trembling on your lips. You want to know what the place is and how old it is and who lived here, don't you?'

Maggy looked surprised. 'Yes, I do, but how did you know?'

'You have an expressive face; besides, I can read your thoughts.' He spoke lightly and plunged into the hotel's history until he was interrupted by the wine waiter. Maggy allowed her gaze to wander once more—it really was delightful, and very smart. She had never been to anything quite like it before, and, she reminded herself soberly, was very unlikely to do so again. She was glad she had on a pretty dress. Would they dance? she wondered. The band seemed good. She turned back to Paul, to find him watching her.

'We'll have a drink, then perhaps you would like to dance?'

The drinks were brought, and she wasn't quite sure what they were.

The doctor raised his glass. 'Champagne cocktail,' he explained, 'to put wings on our feet.'

Maggy didn't need wings. She was a good dancer and as light as a feather despite her size. They were well matched, and circled the floor, not speaking; it didn't seem necessary.

They went back to their table and started a leisurely dinner, and when the waiter removed the remains of the *Sole Normande,* Paul stretched out a hand. 'Let's dance again, shall we?'

Maggy got up at once, her eyes sparkling and her cheeks pink with excitement and the excellent champagne he had chosen. The band was playing a Viennese waltz and they drifted around, scarcely talking. His arm tightened around her and she raised her face to his, smiling, and said, 'I could dance for hours— it's wonderful!'

'You're a beautiful dancer, Maggy.' He was staring down at her.

'And you're a beautiful woman too.' He spoke quietly, without smiling.

Her eyes widened. 'Thank you,' she stammered a little. 'I've never been called beautiful before, it makes a wonderful evening even more wonderful.'

'Don't you believe me?'

She smiled and shook her head. 'No, not really, but it's nice all the same.'

The duckling was everything it should have been, so that it seemed sacrilege to follow it with anything else, but the *bombe bouché aux fruits* was perfection of its kind. When she had eaten the last morsel, Maggy said, 'I'll never forget this dinner, or any moment of this evening.'

'Nor I,' he replied. 'I have seldom enjoyed myself so much. What shall we do, talk or dance?'

'Both,' she answered promptly. 'I should like to know more about the hospital at Leiden.'

He obliged her with a great many interesting details, and she listened absorbed, until he said suddenly,

'You know, it's a great waste of time to talk about work when we could be dancing.' They danced for an hour or more, and if they talked Maggy had no idea what the conversation was about. They were standing waiting for the band to play an encore, when she asked,

'I wonder what the time is?'

Paul looked at his watch. 'Almost twelve.'

'It can't be! We must go home; you have to be in Utrecht by ten tomorrow—you said so.'

The band started up again. He scooped her up neatly, and they were half way round the room before he answered her.

'Plenty of time if I leave Oudehof by eight o'clock.'

'But we're not there yet.'

'What a fearful bully you are, Maggy! We'll go after this dance, provided you promise not to say another word.'

They finished their dance in a companionable silence, and went outside to the car. The night air was cool, and there was plenty of wind, but the sky was clear. Maggy was glad of the soft warmth of the sable coat, despite the warmth of the car. She sat quietly beside Paul, and he didn't speak until they were clear of Baarn.

'Tired?' he asked.

'No, not a bit. It's just so restful sitting here while you drive; and my head's buzzing with the wonderful evening I've had.'

He said he was delighted to hear it, and led the conversation round to her family and home, but while she answered his apparently guileless questions readily enough, she gave him no clue as to where her home actually was. She had told him that it was in the Highlands; but that was a vast, sparsely populated area. He tried again now, but she changed the subject gently but firmly enough for him to be unable to continue with his questions without being guilty of bad manners. He followed her lead, and Maggy sighed with relief. She had made up her mind that when she left Oudehof it would be with no trace of herself left behind.

There was a light in the hall when they returned, Paul got out of the car and opened the big door for her, then said, 'There'll be hot coffee in the kitchen. I'll put the car away while you fill the mugs.'

Maggy waited for the doctor, sitting on the kitchen table, swinging her long shapely legs. She was in a dreamlike state of happiness which she was well aware was only temporary; but the future seemed a long way off at that moment. Paul came in and closed the door quietly behind him, and Maggy slid off the table and poured the coffee, then went and sat sedately in the comfortable old Windsor chair near the stove. The doctor, mug in hand, leaned against the table, watching her. Presently he spoke. 'Shall we go riding before breakfast, Maggy?'

Maggy looked at the old wall clock; it was already three—she didn't feel in the least tired. She agreed happily.

'About seven? Just a quick gallop before you go? I'd like that fine.'

Their eyes met and held and she felt the pink creeping into her cheeks, and hoped he wouldn't see it by the single light she had switched on; she found it impossible to look away.

'Why do you stare so?' she asked at length.

'I'm sorry,' he said quietly. 'I was remembering the night you came down here armed with the poker...'

'Stien was here.' Maggy spoke before she had

thought, and then went on, deliberately giving herself the hurt. 'She is the loveliest girl I have ever seen.'

A look of faint surprise crossed the doctor's face as he answered coolly. 'Yes, she is, isn't she? She will make a most decorative wife.'

Maggy stared down at her mug, the pretty colour fading from her cheeks. She had read a number of novels in which the heroine fell in love with an unresponsive hero, and she now knew exactly how the poor girl felt—only, unlike the girl in the novel, she saw little chance of falling into his arms on the last page.

'You're not listening,' his voice interrupted her unhappy thoughts, and she looked up and said in a bright little voice, unlike hers.

'I'm so sorry.' The change was so sudden that his eyebrows rose in surprise, but before he could comment upon it she stood up.

'I think I'll go to bed. Thank you again for a lovely evening.' Even in her own ears this sounded rather bald, and she cast around for something else to say. 'I expect you go there quite often.'

The doctor was looking at her with narrowed eyes, and answered slowly.

'I think I'll must have taken every girl I ever knew there at some time or other.'

Maggy said, 'Oh!' and scrutinised her nails with care. 'It's a wonderful way to spend an evening.' Her voice was still dreadfully bright.

He agreed, lounging on the table, his eyes on her face.

'Does it surprise you to know that I cannot remember a single girl I took there?'

'Not even Stien?' she asked.

Paul looked puzzled. 'Stien?' He stood up. 'Yes, of course—she being the last of a long line of girls.' He started walking towards Maggy. 'It's strange how, when you meet the woman of your dreams, no one and nothing else matters.'

Maggy listened to his deep voice; he was telling her, very tactfully, that he was going to marry Stien. She would have to go quickly, before she made a fool of herself. She swept the mugs into the sink with the briskness of an early morning east wind, and turned a determinedly cheerful face to him.

'Now I really am going to bed—and I don't think I'll ride in the morning after all. It's so very late, isn't it?' She smiled woodenly and said goodnight and thank you like a well-brought-up child, then went to the door.

Paul was there before her, standing in front of it, searching her face. He looked more arrogant than ever and rather angry as well.

'Ah!' he said softly. 'Maggy is annoyed, and I wonder why, I know of no reason, but I can provide you with one...'

He bent his head, and his mouth came down on hers. His kiss was hard, and without tenderness. She saw the half mocking smile on his lips and ran from the room without a word, scarlet with mortification, trying not to cry.

She didn't sleep. At six o'clock she heard his steps

on the drive outside, and a little later, the sound of Cobber's hooves. She got up and dressed, waited until she heard the Rolls stealing away, and then went downstairs to her breakfast. She wondered if there would be a note...then decided that Paul wasn't the sort of man to leave notes. All the same she looked carefully in all the most likely places, before going sadly upstairs again to re-do her face and put on a bright smile, before going along to Mevrouw Doelsma's room to regale her with a detailed account of her evening out.

CHAPTER NINE

MATRON'S LETTER arrived the next morning, like an answer to Maggy's rather muddled prayers.

It was kind, to the point and brief. Matron wrote to say that if Sister MacFergus could return to duty as soon as possible it would be most convenient, as a number of the nursing staff were off sick... She was hers sincerely, Agatha Humble.

Maggy, that strictly reared member of the Scottish Kirk, was also a true daughter of the Highlands; she could see that Matron's letter was an omen. Without allowing herself more than a few moments' thought of Paul, she sat down at the charming writing desk in her room and answered the letter, assuring Matron that she would return at the earliest time convenient to her patient. Then she went in search of Mevrouw Doelsma and showed her Matron's missive.

Mevrouw Doelsma read it through, dabbed her eyes, and said tearfully,

'Of course you must go, Maggy. I know it's selfish of me to keep you, though I don't know how I'll get on without you; you are so kind and sweet. And what will Paul say?' she went on.

Maggy was half turned away from her, looking out of the windows, across the pleasant gardens. 'I think the doctor knows that I will be returning to England soon.'

'Yes, of course, dear; but surely not as soon as this? When do you suppose you should go?' She looked at her watch. 'Not today, surely? Oh, dear! He will be vexed—he went to Munich to lecture for two days.'

Maggy tried to feel pleased at this news. She need not see him again.

'Then the doctor mustn't be bothered,' she said firmly. 'We…we more or less said goodbye last night. Perhaps I could get a flight tomorrow?'

Mevrouw Doelsma looked at her, began to say something, thought better of it and said, 'Yes, Maggy, of course. Pratt shall ring through to Schiphol and see if they can get you on to a flight. He'll take you down in the car.' She raised a sudden authoritative hand as Maggy started to protest. 'No, I insist. If Paul were here, he would have driven you himself. Now ring for Pratt, please, dear.'

There was a seat on a KLM plane the following evening, Maggy agreed with Mevrouw Doelsma in a rather hollow voice that everything was most satisfactory.

As it was Maggy's last day, her patient insisted that they should go out for a last ride. Maggy drove to Franeker and they visited the Solarium and then went on to Sneek and dawdled between the lakes. The weather was chilly and overcast; the Dutch countryside looked sad—probably at the thought of the cold winter ahead. They arrived back in time for tea, a meal which Mevrouw Doelsma had kept essentially

English, abetted by Mrs Pratt, who had a strong belief that tea was not tea without scones and fruit cake and muffins in their season.

Maggy, pouring tea from the lovely silver pot into the delicate cups, wondered if she would ever enjoy hospital tea again. She packed before dinner, and went to Mevrouw Doelsma's room as was her custom. The little lady pressed a fair-sized box in her hands, and begged her to accept it as a small parting gift. Maggy, who had retained a childish delight in receiving presents, sat down at once and undid the wrappings.

The box contained a soft kid leather handbag; its magnificence rendered her speechless for a moment. She stammered her thanks and Mevrouw Doelsma reached up and kissed her and said, 'There, Maggy, it will last you all your life, and every time you use it, you'll remember me,' and she burst into tears.

Maggy hugged her gently. 'I'll remember you even without your lovely present to remind me.'

'And Paul—will you remember Paul too?'

Maggy managed a smile, and said quite naturally, 'Yes, I shall remember Paul too.'

They played bezique after dinner, until Mevrouw Doelsma declared that she was tired and said goodnight and went up to bed. Once there, however, she went straight to the telephone and dialled her son's home in Leiden. Anny answered and she wasted no words before asking,

'Did Mr Paul leave a telephone number with you, Anny?'

'No, madam. He usually does, but this was only a short trip; but I think I can get a message to the University early tomorrow—he has a lecture there at nine, but he might be able to telephone you before then.'

Mevrouw Doelsma considered this advice and said, 'Yes, do that, Anny. Please tell him that Sister MacFergus is leaving tomorrow evening from Schipol. He could telephone here if he wishes.' She paused. 'You are sure you can get him, aren't you, Anny?'

Anny was sure. 'I can contact the head porter, madam, and he will see that Master Paul gets your message when he arrives.' Mevrouw Doelsma rang off, satisfied.

The doctor arrived in good time to give his lecture. He had, during the course of a wakeful night, decided to leave Munich as soon as was decently possible. There was a dinner that evening which he should attend. He would take an early morning flight to Schipol, telephone Pratt to bring the car to the airport, and go straight to Oudehof. He had to see Maggy.

He went thoughtfully through the imposing doors and looked up, vaguely irritated, as the porter called him by name, and then ran out from his little lodge in the entrance hall. Paul listened to Anny's message without comment, grey eyes staring at the man from a white face. He thanked him politely, asked him to dial a number at Oudehof, just after ten o'clock, when his first lecture would be over, and strode on to the lecture hall, where, with an iron self-control which did not allow of his thoughts straying to Maggy, he delivered one of the best lectures he had ever given.

He was in the consultants' room, talking quietly with a group of doctors, when his call came through. He took it in a quiet corner of the room, away from the others.

Pratt's voice came, clear and rather thin, over the wire. 'Mr Paul? I'll fetch Madam at once.'

The doctor said quietly, 'Wait, Pratt. Please find Sister MacFergus, and ask her to speak to me, and send someone to ask my mother to come to the telephone meanwhile. Hurry, will you? I have only a few minutes.'

He sat patiently until he heard his mother's voice.

'Paul? They're looking for Maggy. She's leaving just after lunch, and catching the eight o'clock plane. I—I tried to stop her, dear.'

'Don't worry, Mother; I'm sure you did all you could.'

'Yes, I did, Paul. But when Maggy told me that you'd already said goodbye and that you would understand why she was going, there wasn't much I could say.'

'No, of course not, dearest.' He spoke slowly, looking at the wall in front of him, remembering Maggy's soft lips under his.

'Pratt's here,' his mother told him. 'No one can find Maggy. Perhaps she is out.' She sounded doubtful.

The doctor looked at the clock on the wall before him. He had less than three minutes before the next lecture; the room was emptying already. He spoke unhurriedly.

'Mother, will you tell Maggy to wait in the reception hall at Schipol. I'll try and get a seat on the early evening plane from here. I believe it gets in thirty minutes before her flight leaves—No, that's not enough time; ask her to transfer to the ten o'clock flight.'

He said goodbye, hung up and went back to the lecture hall; pausing at the lodge to tell the porter to get him a seat on the plane leaving Munich just before five o'clock that afternoon.

Maggy hated saying goodbye; it was with a feeling almost of relief that she saw the last of Oudehof as Pratt drove through the gates on to the main road and turned the car towards the Afsluitdijk. It was, he declared, the quickest way to the airport, even if not the prettiest. It was a sad, grey day, and Maggy's face reflected the sadness. Pratt, a kindly man, did his best to maintain a cheerful conversation, and Maggy realising it, answered him civilly in an unhappy voice, telling herself that none of it was true, and that presently she would wake up and find herself back in her bedroom at Oudehof.

They got to Schiphol with almost an hour to spare. Pratt shepherded her past authority, found her a seat in the reception hall, and wished her a reluctant farewell, adding the fervent hope that they would all be seeing her again before very long. She shook his hand and laughed a little and said,

'I think that is most unlikely, Pratt, but I shall remember these few weeks all my life, and Mrs Pratt's
and your kind help to me.'

She watched his elderly back disappearing through
the door, and felt suddenly very lonely. He was her
last link with Paul. She looked at her watch; she had
almost half an hour before her plane left; the doctor's
flight was due in fifteen minutes. Not very long for
her to decide how to avoid him. When Mevrouw
Doelsma had given her his message, she had realised
at once that she must not see him again. She had
heard Pratt and Mrs Pratt calling to her that morning
because the doctor was on the phone and wanted to
speak to her, and she had stayed quiet in the stable
with Cobber, longing to go. She had no idea what he
would or what he could want to say to her; only she
wanted to hear his voice, just once more.

Now she looked around her. There were a great
many people milling around—late holidaymakers;
business men; a small group of nuns, even a party of
uniformed schoolgirls in charge of a harassed teacher.
Maggy walked slowly towards them, wishing that it
was time to board the plane. The temptation to go to
the desk and get a transfer to the later plane was very
strong, but she fought it back; there was no point in
seeing Paul again. She looked nervously at the clock,
then at her watch, and saw with a kind of despair that
it wanted a minute to the half-hour. There was a plane
circling to land—it touched down as she watched
from the window; that would be Paul's plane. She

would be gone by the time he had cleared Customs and reached the departure hall.

In sudden panic she visualised him finding her before she could get away, and turned to see the long straggling queue, already spilling back into the hall from the pier leading to her gate. The hall seemed very empty. If she took her place at the back of the queue now, he would be sure to see her; she had her wretched size to thank for that certainty. She looked at the clock again; ten minutes had gone by, but the obedient crocodile was still standing patiently, waiting for the gate to open. There had been a delay perhaps, some small hitch; just enough to spoil her careful, unhappy planning. She wasted precious seconds, imagining Paul coming through the doors at the far end of the hall, and seeing her—and saying what? She only had to stay where she was to find out...

Maggy turned with a resolution she was far from feeling. She had to get to the head of the queue; she could see the gate at the far end of the pier. It was still shut, almost obscured by a bevy of navy blue school hats. She began to weave her way through the waiting passengers—a slow business with frequent pauses while she explained that she was travelling with the school party in front. She reached her goal at last, and smiled with such friendliness and relief at the schoolteacher that the worried little woman imagined that she must be someone she had met at some time, and smiled back and even made a remark about the delay, so that those in the queue behind who suspected Maggy of jumping the line decided that they had been mistaken after all. The man at the gate shared their views too, and told Maggy cheerfully that the girls would soon be safely on board—the delay wouldn't last more than another ten minutes or so.

Maggy stood very still, not daring to turn around, realising sickeningly that by some stroke of fate she stood head and shoulders above her immediate neighbours. It was five past eight when the gate opened, and the first reluctant schoolgirl went through. Maggy looked back. Paul was approaching the pier; he looked immense and confident, and rather arrogant, even at that distance. He looked at her over the heads of the people between them. Their eyes met for a long moment before she turned quickly, showed her ticket, and walked as fast as possible to the waiting plane.

Paul watched the big KLM plane glide down the runway and waited until it was a speck in the grey, darkening sky, before he made his way to a telephone booth and rang Pratt. Having done this, he went and sat down, outwardly composed and patient, waiting for him to bring the Rolls back to the airport.

He replied to Pratt's greeting with a brief grunt, then took the wheel himself and drove the short distance to Leiden at a speed which left his faithful friend and servant speechless. His house reached, Paul left Pratt to put the car away and went indoors, throwing his coat and gloves on to a chair as he strode through the hall to his study. A few minutes later, Pratt, on his way to the kitchen, was arrested by his master's imperative voice demanding his presence, and made haste to answer the summons. The doctor was at his desk, unlocking a drawer.

'Pratt, I shall want the car to take to England on tomorrow night's Hoek boat. See about tickets and all the necessary papers, will you? Telephone Mijnheer Felman at his house and ask him to arrange it, and get that man—what was his name—to see to the insurance.'

'The name is Mulder, sir. Shall I collect them for you tomorrow?'

Pratt was already dialling a number. Dr Doelsma put his passport in his pocket and walked across to the wall safe concealed behind a small picture on it. He selected a key from the bunch in his hand, and opened the safe door, felt around inside and withdrew a small leather bag, which he transferred to a pocket; it took him a little longer to find a small leather-covered case. He opened it, and stood looking at the magnificent sapphire and diamond ring, before closing it, and transferring it likewise to the same pocket. He stood deep in thought until Pratt had finished telephoning, then said,

'Will you get hold of the Customs people first thing in the morning? I want to take the Van Beijnen pearls and a ring to England. They will be brought back within a few days. Arrange it, will you, Pratt? I'll let you have their description, and leave you a blank cheque.'

Pratt inclined his head. 'I'll see to it, sir. Mijnheer Mulder will have everything ready by about three o'clock tomorrow afternoon.'

The doctor had seated himself at his desk, and was checking his appointments book. 'I shall want Anny to pack a few things, too,' he said.

'For how long will you be gone, sir?'

The doctor met Pratt's fatherly eye with his own grey ones, and said blandly, 'That depends entirely upon Miss MacFergus. I daresay I shall telephone you within a day or so.'

Pratt allowed his elderly features to break into a smile. 'Just so, sir,' he said in a satisfied voice. Paul looked up from his desk again.

'Don't go, Pratt. Do I not have an uncle who has a slight acquaintance with the Archbishop of Canterbury?'

Pratt, who knew the doctor's family history as well as he did himself, had only to think for a moment.

'Indeed you have, sir. Your Great-Uncle Bartholomew on your mother's side. He is, if you remember, a Bishop, and must, I feel sure, carry some weight in ecclesiastical circles. I gather it is a special marriage licence you have in mind, sir?'

Dr Doelsma leaned back and surveyed the older man with twinkling eyes. His earlier rage had entirely disappeared.

'You gather correctly, Pratt, as always. How long will it take?'

'I suggest you telephone the Bishop now, sir. He should be able to expedite the matter.'

The doctor got up. 'Get him for me, will you, Pratt? I shall be in the kitchen; I want a word with Anny.'

Anny was sitting in her easy chair by the Aga,

reading a magazine. She put it down as Paul entered the room, and started to get up, but he pushed her back with a gentle hand, helped himself to a slice of cake from the kitchen table, and drew up a chair to sit by her.

The housekeeper looked at him severely. 'What about your dinner, Mr Paul? Done to a turn when you got in, and you went straight to the study.'

He looked rather blankly at her. 'I forgot, Anny.' He munched his cake.

'So you missed Miss Maggy, sir.'

He reached for another piece of cake. 'Yes, Anny, I did. But not, I fancy, through any fault of mine. I shall be going over to England tomorrow. Can I leave you to see that the master bedroom is prepared for our return?'

Anny settled her glasses more firmly on her nose, 'It'll be a real pleasure, Master Paul...'

She was interrupted by the telephone and Paul went to answer it. It was Uncle Bartholomew, who wasted several minutes discussing his arthritis, but once Paul had explained what he wanted became extremely businesslike. Paul put down the receiver at length, to encounter Anny's eyes, round with excitement.

'Do you know where Sister MacFergus is, sir?' she asked.

He stood up. 'No, Anny. I don't, but if I have the licence, we can marry wherever we meet.' He waved an airy hand, and disappeared, leaving her with her unopened magazine on her lap; her thoughts were far more interesting.

It took most of the evening to arrange for clinics and lectures to be taken by colleagues—his own patients he persuaded Dr Bennink to take over for a few days. He would have to make time to go to the hospital in the morning, before he went to Oudehof to see his mother. It was quite late when he sat down to a supper insisted upon by Anny; he sat over it a long time, thinking about Maggy.

St Ethelburga's looked grey and rather grim as Paul drew up on the courtyard the following afternoon. He got out of the car and went inside, and old George, recognising him at once, said, 'There's a letter for you, sir. Is it Sir Charles Warren you wanted to see?'

Paul asked if he might have a few minutes of the Matron's time, and while George was ringing her office, examined the entirely satisfactory contents of the envelope. Great-Uncle Bartholomew had certainly lost no time.

If Matron was surprised to see the doctor, she showed no sign of it, and it was only after a few minutes of polite conversation that she enquired if she could do anything for him. Paul shifted his bulk cautiously on the small chair. 'I should like to see Sister MacFergus, if that is possible, Matron.'

She looked faintly surprised. 'But Sister only returned from Holland the day before yesterday.'

Her tone implied that he had had ample opportunity to see her there should he have wished. 'She was due some leave, and she didn't look at all her usual self.

I need her badly here, but I advised her to go to her home for a week or two.'

'May I have her address?' he asked abruptly.

Matron hesitated. 'I suppose so. Sister MacFergus made no mention of you coming...'

'I don't suppose she did,' he answered easily. 'She didn't know.'

'If I don't give it to you, Dr Doelsma, I suppose you will find someone who will—'

'Most certainly I shall, Matron.' He smiled charmingly at her.

'Very well. Her parents live in the factor's house on Aultostish estate in Inverness-shire—her father is factor to the laird.' She added dryly, 'It's about six hundred miles from here.'

He stood up. 'Fortunately I brought the car over with me. Thank you for your help, Matron. Before I go, might I visit Mrs Salt for a moment? There is something I must tell her.'

Matron nodded dumbly, wondering what on earth he could have to say to old Mrs Salt on Women's Medical. 'Can you find the way, or shall I get a porter?'

Paul held out his hand. 'I'll find my own way; and thank you again.'

Mrs Salt didn't seem very surprised to see him. She waited until he was standing by the bed and then said, ''Ullo. I thought yer'd be 'ere. Sister came to see me. Wot yer done to 'er? She don't look 'erself no more.' She frowned fiercely at him.

He sat down beside her and said gently, 'I'm not

quite sure, Mrs Salt, but whatever it was it wasn't intentional. I'm on my way to see her now.'

'Ho, are yer?' The old lady spoke belligerently.

Paul ignored her cross tone, but went on, 'We shall both be here for your birthday.'

'Are yer goin' ter marry 'er?' Mrs Salt smiled for the first time.

He got up. 'Yes, Mrs Salt, before your birthday. Goodbye.' He enchanted her by lifting one of her bony hands and kissing it.

He left the car where it was and took a taxi to Simpson's, and over lunch mapped out his route. By three o'clock he was threading his way through London's suburbia, the Rolls' elegant nose pointing north. He eased the car through Welwyn, confident of making up time on the motorway ahead. He was however doomed to disappointment; an accident some way ahead had closed the road before him for some miles. Paul sat calmly at the wheel showing no sign of his raging impatience. When at last the road was clear again, he had lost almost an hour.

He drove on steadily, barely noticing the towns through which he passed—St Neots; Stamford; Grantham—and skimmed up the motorway beyond Doncaster. He had done almost a quarter of his journey, and it was seven o'clock, and he was hungry. But he didn't stop for another hour, when he pulled in for petrol at Scotch Corner and had a quick meal at the hotel, poring over his maps, committing the road to his excellent memory. With luck on his side, he should be at Maggy's home soon after breakfast. He wasn't tired; the whole of his strength and energy was concentrated on reaching her at the earliest possible moment.

It was almost nine o'clock when he set off again; four hours later he was going through Edinburgh, still with two hundred miles to go. Probably the last part of the journey would be over difficult country. He crossed the Forth Bridge, and took the A9 to Perth. It was a brilliant night, with a small slice of moon dangling amongst the stars. The road started to climb steadily; he was on the fringe of the Highlands, and there was almost no traffic. The Rolls tore ahead with effortless speed. Paul touched a switch, and the hood sank back, leaving the cold night air to rush at him; he welcomed its tonic chill, and began to whistle softly.

Paul made his way through a sleeping Perth, and on to Inverness. It was six o'clock and growing light. He stopped for petrol and found a hotel open nearby, where he shaved and washed and drank several cups of coffee while he listened to the careful instruction of the night porter. He went on out of the town, the man's directions ringing in his ears. The porter had been right; the road was a good one as far as Garve, but after that he was forced to slow his pace as he crossed the river and turned up the small hilly road to Aultdearg. He was going very slowly now, so that he would not miss the narrow dirt road which would lead him to the factor's house.

There was a wall marching with the road now, and rounding a corner Paul saw the house, tucked into the

side of the lane, with its back to the hills. It looked
square and solid and welcoming in the early morning
sun. Paul stopped the car at its gate and looked at his
watch; it was nine o'clock. He got out of the car and
walked slowly up the flag-stone path to the front door.
The knocker was large and old-fashioned and highly
polished. It echoed through the quietness around and
was finally answered by the brisk opening of a window above the doctor's head. A woman, with
Maggy's eyes and Maggy's hair, looked down at him
and then at the Rolls, travel-stained but still magnificent, standing at the gate.

Dr Doelsma smiled, 'Mrs MacFergus? I've come
to see Maggy.'

'Aye, and a long way, by the look of ye, Doctor.
I'll be down to let ye in.' She returned his smile, and
disappeared, to stand before him a moment later,
holding the door open.

'Maggy's out with the dogs,' she said. 'Will ye
have breakfast now, and wait here?'

The doctor smiled again. 'I'll own I'm hungry, but
if you would tell me where I can find her—?'

Maggy's mother twinkled at him. 'She's gone up
the hill path at the back of the house—it'll stretch
your legs nicely for you after the long sit ye've had
in that car.'

She led him through the house and out into the
garden beyond, where there was a gate opening on to
a field of rough grass leading up to the wooded hills
beyond. He could see the rough path winding up be-

tween the trees before it disappeared around the brow of the nearest hill, misty with threatening rain.

Maggy came over the crest of the hill, walking slowly, the dogs weaving to and fro before her, trying to attract her attention. There had been a singular lack of sticks thrown, to be caught and brought back. Maggy did not care about sticks; occasionally she said 'Good dog' or 'Go, seek,' in an absent-minded fashion, but her heart wasn't in it, and the dogs knew this. She was suffering from the bitter after-taste of something done which, however right, was against personal inclination.

She plodded on in her elderly kilt and thick sweater. The drizzle had covered her in a fine spangle of silvery drops, and the wind had whipped her hair into feathery curls. She was contemplating a day stretching emptily ahead of her, followed by other days, all equally empty. For the hundredth time she thought of Paul. The dogs gave tongue, and Maggy abandoned her hopeless dreams to stand and look around her. Coming towards her down the other side of the glen was the doctor, covering the ground rapidly with long easy strides.

Maggy closed her eyes, and then looked again. He was still there. She stood, stunned by the fact that her dreams had all at once become reality. It was extraordinary how the mist-covered hills around her had suddenly become Paradise. She started to run down the narrow path, her heart racing in time with her feet, the dogs running on either side. The doctor had stopped and stood watching her headlong flight, to open his arms and catch her close as she reached him, apparently unshaken by the onslaught of six feet of well-rounded girl.

Maggy said into his shoulder, 'Paul! Oh, Paul! I wanted you to come so much, and you came.'

Paul tightened an arm around her, and if he found this remark, in the light of recent events, rather puzzling, he made no comment. Instead he said, 'My dear girl, naturally I came.' There was a ghost of a laugh in his voice.

'How did you find me?' She looked up at him, suddenly feeling shy. He didn't answer, but kissed her mouth with a sudden fierceness that left her breathless. When she could speak again, she said,

'I didn't mean you to find me, Paul.'

His eyes twinkled. 'My dearest goose, did you really think that a mere seven or eight hundred miles would keep me from following you?' He kissed her again, gently. 'My delightful Maggy, you have no idea what a nuisance you have been to me; do you know that I have left patients and lectures and clinics in the unwilling laps of half the medical profession in Leiden?'

'I'm sorry, Paul…do you find me very silly?'

He kissed her again in a reassuring fashion. 'No, darling. Only I don't know why you needed to run away. You're not afraid of me?'

Maggy raised an astonished face. 'Afraid of you? Paul, how could I be afraid of you when I love you?'

Paul looked at her tenderly. 'Then why, my dearest?'

'I—I didn't think you loved me…at least, once or twice I thought perhaps you did, a little, and then that night when we went out and we were talking in the kitchen and you told me about the girls you had taken out and you said that Stien would make a decorative wife…'

'So I did,' Paul agreed, 'but I don't remember saying that she was going to be my wife.'

Maggy said rather crossly, 'No, of course you didn't; but she's in Utrecht, and you practically live there.'

The grey eyes opened wide and stared down at her. 'My love, my bad-tempered little love! I have set eyes on Stien just once since she was at Oudehof, and that was when she asked me to give her a lift to a party in Utrecht because her car had broken down. I go to Utrecht because I have a home for old people there. You see, Maggy, I have a great deal of money…I bought an old house and converted it…it has taken up much of my time. But not,' he added softly, 'as much as you.' He kissed her again. 'Is that why you couldn't be found when I telephoned Oudehof from Munich?' Maggy nodded into his shoulder. 'And avoided me so cleverly at Schiphol?' he went on. Maggy nodded again.

'Will you marry me, my darling? Very soon, before you get any more ideas into your head. There is, I know, a lot of explaining to do, but I think I prefer to do it at my leisure, in the comfort of our own home.'

They smiled at each other. 'It will be very nice to

come home in the evening,' said Paul, 'and find you waiting.'

He kissed her again, with an urgency that left her pink-cheeked and shaking, so that he held her gently while he said the things she had longed to hear him say. Neither of them noticed the thickening drizzle. After a time the patient dogs, at last grown impatient, got up and shook themselves, and trotted off into the trees, their tongues lolling. They looked back once as they went, but neither Paul nor Maggy had seen them go.

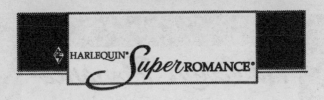

...there's more to the story!

Superromance.
A *big* satisfying read about unforgettable characters. Each month we offer *six* very different stories that range from family drama to adventure and mystery, from highly emotional stories to romantic comedies—and much more! Stories about people you'll believe in and care about. Stories too compelling to put down....

Our authors are among today's *best* romance writers. You'll find familiar names and talented newcomers. Many of them are award winners—and you'll see why!

If you want the biggest and best in romance fiction, you'll get it from Superromance!

Emotional, Exciting, Unexpected...

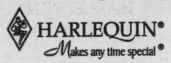

HARLEQUIN®
Makes any time special ®

HARLEQUIN *Presents*

The world's bestselling romance series...
The series that brings you your favorite authors,
month after month:

Helen Bianchin...Emma Darcy
Lynne Graham...Penny Jordan
Miranda Lee...Sandra Marton
Anne Mather...Carole Mortimer
Susan Napier...Michelle Reid

and many more uniquely talented authors!

Wealthy, powerful, gorgeous men...
Women who have feelings just like your own...
The stories you love, set in exotic, glamorous locations...

HARLEQUIN *Presents*

Seduction and passion guaranteed!

HARLEQUIN®
INTRIGUE

WE'LL LEAVE YOU BREATHLESS!

If you've been looking for thrilling tales of
contemporary passion and sensuous love stories
with taut, edge-of-the-seat suspense—then
you'll love Harlequin Intrigue!

Every month, you'll meet four new heroes
who are guaranteed to make your spine tingle
and your pulse pound. With them you'll enter
into the exciting world of Harlequin Intrigue—
where your life is on the line
and so is your heart!

THAT'S INTRIGUE—
ROMANTIC SUSPENSE
AT ITS BEST!

HARLEQUIN®
Makes any time special ®

Harlequin® Historical

From rugged lawmen and valiant knights to defiant heiresses and spirited frontierswomen, Harlequin Historicals will capture your imagination with their dramatic scope, passion and adventure.

Harlequin Historicals...
they're too good to miss!

HHDIR1